DR. DEVO'S
LiCKETY-
SPLiT
DEVOTIONS

Zonder**kidz**™

The children's group of Zondervan

www.zonderkidz.com

Dr. Devo's Lickety-Split Devotions
Copyright © 2002 by Tim Wesemann

Requests for information should be addressed to:
Grand Rapids, Michigan 49530

ISBN: 0–310–70355–7

Editor: Barbara J. Scott
Interior design: Laura Maitner and Amy E. Langeler
Art direction: Jody Langley

Printed in the United States of America

02 03 04 05 06 07 /❖DC/ 10 9 8 7 6 5 4 3 2 1

DR. DEVO'S LICKETY-SPLIT DEVOTIONS

by Tim Wesemann
illustrations by Dana Thompson

Zonderkidz

Lickety–Split Love To:
Jesus,
Christopher,
Sarah,
Benjamin,
and Chiara

**Your word is a lamp to my feet and
a light for my path.**
Psalm 119:105

Give me a sense of humor, Lord,
Give me the grace to see a joke,
To get some humor out of life
And pass it on to other folk.
—Anonymous

Special thanks to:
my home editors, readers,
helpers & pray-ers—
especially Linda, Ulricke, and the
Zawadzki family; the 3rd, 4th, & 5th
graders at Salem Lutheran School in
Affton, Missouri (2001-2002 school year),
and the Zonderkidz team,
especially Barbara and Gary.

Dr. Devo's
Lickety-Split
Table of Contents

Do you know what lickety-split means? Choose one of these answers.

a fast **b** fast **c** fast **d** a, b, & c

Quick! I need your answer now! That's right—the answer is d. Looks like you're no slacker. Now that we've covered that, let me introduce myself.

I'm Dr. Devo (short for DEVOtions, of course) and this is a book of lickety-split (fast, fast, fast) and fun, fun, fun devotions. Why so fast? Well, check out this verse:

> It is the Lord your God you must follow, and him you must revere. Keep his commands and obey him; serve him and hold fast to him.
>
> DEUTERONOMY 13:4

God wants us to hold fast to him and his words in the Bible. Actually, "holding fast" has nothing to do with speed. It means "being true to him" or "united with him." Following Jesus is fun! Hold fast to the Lord and hold on tight, because we'll be going lickety-split as we learn to love the Savior who came to save us!

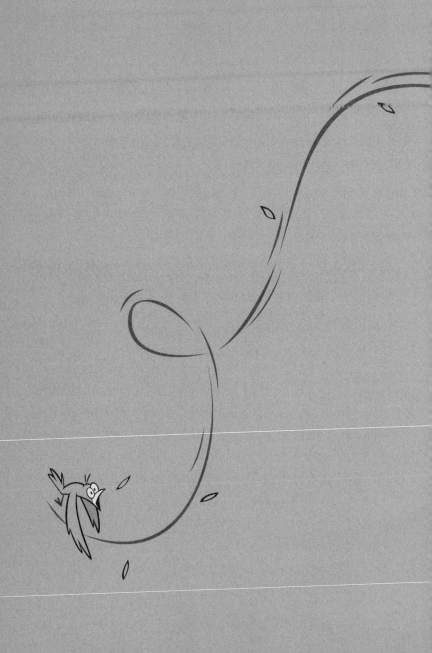

Weekday Devotions

THANKS FOR THE MANNA FLAKES

Do you like eating the same cereal every day?

God's Old Testament people traveled in the wilderness for forty years. They complained because God was feeding them the same breakfast every day—something called manna, which means, "What is it?" It fell from the sky while they slept. They'd wake up and say, "What is it?"

They could have made fun meals out of manna. Think of the possibilities: bamanna bread, hamanna sandwiches, scrambled manna, fried manna, bamanna splits!

But the people complained. Maybe they said, "Manna, manna, every day. Give us something chickens lay!" God was doing great things for them but they missed his blessings by being ungrateful.

Don't miss the great things God is doing in your life! Start by enjoying and thanking God for the food he provides for you today. Then look around and thank God for all his gifts! Say this as you start your day:

> The LORD has done great things for us, and we are filled with joy.
> **PSALM 126:3**

FOR CRYING OUT LOUD!

Animals don't cry—but humans do.

Still, there are plenty of things I don't understand about crying. Maybe you can help me out.

1. When we get hurt, why do we try so hard not to cry in front of other people—even if it really hurts?

2. Why is it easier to cry around our moms than our dads?

3. What are those funny little gasps that come out of us after we stop crying?

4. Don't you think it's great that we can also cry when we're happy?

5. Why did Jesus cry?

Jesus cried? Yep, and he cried in front of other people. He didn't hide it. When Jesus' friend Lazarus died, the Bible says:

> **Jesus wept. Then the Jews said,
> "See how he loved him!"**
> JOHN 11:35-36

Jesus knows what it's like to be sad.

God created us with emotions and he gave us tears to relieve our sadness. If you feel like having a good cry today—go ahead! Jesus understands. He can make you feel better!

ARE YOU WIDE AWAKE?

According to NATIONAL GEOGRAPHIC, in an average lifetime the average American blinks 393,674,400 times. That means, if indeed you are "average," your eyes are shut for:

a 4 months   **b** 9 months   **c** 18 months

The answer is *c*—eighteen months. Wow! In a lifetime, you would be missing out on seeing a year and a half's worth of stuff! And that doesn't count sleeping! That's another twenty-four years of shut-eye!

The Bible says:

Let us not be like the others. They are asleep. Instead, let us be wide awake and in full control of ourselves.

1 THESSALONIANS 5:6 NIrV

That doesn't mean God doesn't want us to sleep or blink! But he does want us to be awake and aware of the temptations to sin that surround us—from classmates, friends, songs, TV, movies. We can't spend our lives huddling under the bed. So we must stay awake and alert so we can say, "No!" to those things that draw us away from God.

FACE-OFF

If you're all in a good mood, this will be fun and easy. If you're not very happy today, well, this may be just what you need! I call it the Dr. Devo face-off.

Here are the instructions.

1. Each person has one opportunity to make a funny face.

2. The other contestants judge the face on a scale of one to ten, based on creativity and form. You cannot vote for yourself.

3. The winner doesn't have to clean up after supper for the next two days.

Let the face-off begin!

I hope that brought you lots of laughs! The Bible talks about God's face. It says:

> **Seek his face always.**
> 1 CHRONICLES 16:11

Our days will be so much happier if we constantly look to God's face of joy and love.

Face the facts: God wants us to always look to him for help, forgiveness, love, fun, power, and every other good gift he has for us. Face it—he loves you very much!

WHERE DO YOU LIVE?

Below are names of real towns. Try to match the city with the state where it is located.

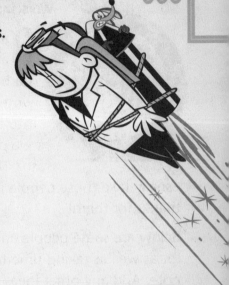

1. Lizard Lick _C_
2. Noodle _A_
3. Joe _B_
4. Sweet Lips _H_
5. Tightwad _D_
6. Nothing _G_
7. Zap _F_
8. Monkey's Eyebrow _E_

States: *(a)* Texas, *(b)* Montana, *(c)* North Carolina, *(d)* Missouri, *(e)* Kentucky, *(f)* North Dakota, *(g)* Arizona, *(h)* Tennessee.

When the children of Israel left Egypt and headed for the Promised Land, they camped in the Desert of Sin (read Exodus 16:1–2). That doesn't sound like the best place to camp, does it? But many times we camp out in the middle of sin—even though we know what's right and what's wrong.

If you've been camping in the Desert of Sin, it may be time to move your tent to a place called Mount Calvary. That's where Jesus died on the cross to take away our sins. And remember, Mount Calvary has a great view of heaven!

Is there anything in your life that you need to ask God to forgive you for?

Answers: 1-c, 2-a, 3-b, 4-h, 5-d, 6-g, 7-f, 8-e.

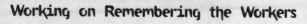

Working on Remembering the Workers

Have you ever thanked the men and women who pick up your garbage? If not, maybe you could write them a note of thanks and tape it to the garbage can. Can you imagine if we didn't have people to pick up our trash? That's a stinky thought! But we usually take those people for granted. We should give thanks for them!

Below are some people and jobs we can start thanking God for as well as taking time to thank them in person or with a note. Add any other ideas you have.

- garbage collectors
- mail carriers
- nurses
- salespeople
- janitors
- bank tellers
- road workers
- plumbers
- church secretaries

Many times we take the work of God in our lives for granted as well. Take a moment to thank him for helping you become all you were created to be.

As you think about it, remember that God says:

> **Whatever you do, work at it with all your heart, as working for the Lord, not for men.**
> **COLOSSIANS 3:23**

16

UPS AND DOWNS

We all have up days and down days.

Feeling great. Feeling lousy. Up and down. Happy, then sad. Up. Down. Feeling close to God. Feeling like he is far away.

Having a close relationship with Jesus, always praising him, and finding our joy in him would be wonderful. But none of us is perfect and we live in a sinful world. We're going to have those ups and downs. Thankfully, Jesus doesn't. His love for us stays constant, helping us through tough times and reminding us to rejoice in the good times.

During the up and down times, remember what Paul wrote:

I am convinced that neither death nor life, neither angels nor demons, neither the present nor the future, nor any powers, neither height nor depth, nor anything else in all creation, will be able to separate us from the love of God that is in Christ Jesus our Lord.
ROMANS 8:38-39

I hope that good news raises you up to new heights today!

GET THE RIGHT INSTRUCTIONS

Here's my recipe [with exact instructions] for making a peanut butter and jelly sandwich:

1. Take two slices of bread and place them side by side.

2. Remove the lid to the grape jelly. With a knife, take some jelly out of the jar—enough to cover the surface of one slice of bread. Spread it on one side of a slice of bread.

3. Repeat step 2, but this time with peanut butter. Put the peanut butter on the other slice of bread.

4. Put the knife down and place the bread slices together. Enjoy!

Did I miss anything? Oh yes!

When telling you to put the bread slices together, I didn't say to put the ingredients on the inside! That might seem obvious, but what if you had never seen a peanut butter and jelly sandwich before?

When you tell others about Jesus, remember to share all the important things. Don't leave anything out—even if it seems obvious. Before your family prayer today, read and discuss the following verse.

Always be prepared to give an answer to everyone who asks you to give the reason for the hope that you have.
1 PETER 3:15

18

Hey, Dr. Devo Dude,

I got this, like, question for you, man. My older brother has some friends who smoke cigarettes. My bro doesn't smoke but he hangs with them. Sometimes they ask me if, like, I want a smoke. I say no but I'm curious. Would it be, like, totally wrong if I smoked?

Signed,

Cig Dude

Dear Cig Dude,

If you're, like, smokin', dude, hit the ground and roll— that means you're on fire! Seriously, check out what that Bible dude, Paul, wrote: "Do you not know that your body is a temple of the Holy Spirit? . . . You are not your own; you were bought at a price. Therefore honor God with your body" (1 Corinthians 6:19–20).

There's your answer, dude. Would putting tar and nicotine and smoke in your body be a way of honoring God? What are other things you could put in your body that would not honor God? Smoking is a dud, dude!

Signed,

Dr. Devo— on fire for God

Did you know that there's something you can break this morning and you won't get into trouble?

You ou can start with breaking out of a sleepy, grumpy mood by breaking into a smile. That's a great way to start your day! But you can also break your fast. While you've been sleeping, your body has been fasting. Do you know what a fast is?

When the Bible tells of someone fasting, it's taking a break from eating (and sometimes drinking). It's a kind of sacrifice and devotion. When someone gives up a meal, they're supposed to take that time and use it to pray or study God's Word.

We can't eat and sleep at the same time. We wake up and "break the fast" by eating breakfast. It may not be a true fast, because we aren't praying or studying God's Word, but we are doing what God wants us to do. We're taking care of the bodies he's blessed us with, by refueling our bodies after we rest—a very important part of God's plan for us.

WHAT DO YOU THINK?

We spend most of our day thinking, but the things we think about are often negative, bad, and sinful.

Don't you think that is because we think that if we don't act on or say the things we are thinking, they aren't really wrong or sinful? What do you think?

In Philippians 4:8–9 Paul encouraged God's people to think about good things. Below is a list of words from the Bible verse. List things to think about that fit the description of the word. Paul said to think about whatever is . . .

true
_____

noble
_____

right
_____

pure
_____

lovely
_____

admirable
_____

excellent
_____

praiseworthy
_____

Dear Jesus, help me to think on things that are true, noble, right, pure, lovely, admirable, excellent, and praiseworthy. I love you. Amen.

YOU CAN DO IT! BUT HOW?

An ant can lift fifty times its own weight.

Do you have an aunt (or uncle) that can do that? God also made bees to handle three hundred times their own weight! Humans can't lift that much, nor do we need to—unless God needs us to for a special reason.

The Bible says:

> I can do everything through him
> who gives me strength.
>
> PHILIPPIANS 4:13

That's an amazing promise. But by using the word *everything,* Paul is saying, "everything that is pleasing to God." Not all things give God the glory or please him. We want to do his will. Normally we wouldn't need to handle something three hundred times our weight. But if it accomplishes his purposes, he can make it possible.

It's a great promise to remember: we can do all things that are pleasing to God, through Jesus Christ, who will give us the strength. That's amazing, incredible, and it's just like our God to leave us with such a powerful promise—don't forget that!

WHO'S WHO?

It's time for a Dr. Devo multiple-guess pop quiz!

Question 1: What do the following people have in common: Malachi Kittredge, Orval Overall, Squiz Pillon, Ossie Schreckengost, and Yats Wuestling?

a. They all ruled Germany.

b. They all claim to have invented the toilet.

c. They all played major-league baseball.

Question 2: What do the following people have in common: Salmon, Amon, Azor, Zadok, and Matthan?

a. They built Solomon's temple.

b. They were all Israelite judges.

c. They were part of Jesus' family tree.

The answer to both questions is c. Check Matthew 1:1–17 about question 2.

You probably hadn't heard of those people. You can know for sure that even if people don't know you or remember you, God knows you, loves you, and has a plan for your life.

FACE-OFF

"I know the plans I have for you," declares the Lord, "plans to prosper you and not to harm you, plans to give you hope and a future."

JEREMIAH 29:11

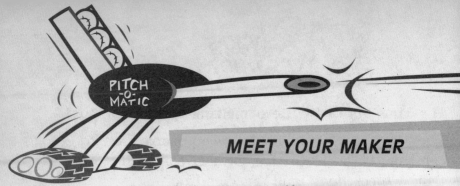

Here comes a Dr. Devo lickety-split pop quiz!

Question 1: Which of the following did Thomas Edison invent?

a. the electric light

b. the motion-picture camera

c. wax paper

d. an electric railway car

e. the radio vacuum tube

f. all of the above

Question 2: What did God create?

a. all of the above

b. all of the below

c. all around

d. *a, b,* and *c*

The answer to question 1 is *f*. The answer to question 2 is *d*.

Thomas Edison was one of the greatest inventors ever. Many of his inventions changed the way we do things today. But there is a much greater creator—the only true God.

He created everything in the universe. It's easy to take his creation for granted. Take our bodies, for example. Right now our minds are thinking, hearts are beating, blood is pumping, and our eyelids are blinking.

Constantly thank God for his creation!

24

DR. DEVO'S ADVICE COLUMN

Dear Dr. Devo,

My hero is the quarterback of the St. Louis Rams football team. He is so cool. I want to be just like him. Sports players hardly ever answer their mail, so I haven't written him. I don't know his phone number to talk to him. I can imitate his passing style perfectly. I even cut my hair to look like his. What do you think about my hero?

Signed,

Ram Sacked

Dear Ram Sacked,

It's okay to have heroes—just remember that they can let us down. Athletes aren't perfect. There is only one person who is. His name is Jesus and he's head of his Father's team.

He is someone to imitate. (See Ephesians 5:1.) And while you're doing that, enjoy watching your favorite football team. But don't put your faith in people. Rather imitate the greatest hero who didn't just save a game—he saved the world!

God's blessings,

Dr. Devo

Missionaries

Question 1: How do you communicate with a fish?

Answer: Drop it a line.

Question 2: How can you communicate with a missionary in a foreign land?

Answer: Drop them a line—by mail, e-mail, or prayer mail!

Missionaries need to know people are praying for them. Your church probably has the names and addresses of missionaries you could pray for. When you pray, it is also a great idea to drop them a line to let them know you are praying for them. Ask them about specific prayer requests they have that you can pray for in the future. Here are some prayer ideas to start with.

➡ safety
➡ new ways to share the good news of Jesus
➡ good health
➡ homesickness
➡ money concerns
➡ the government where they serve

The missionary Paul wrote the members of the church in the city of Thessalonica and simply said:

> **Brothers, pray for us.**
>
> **1 THESSALONIANS 5:25**

Take turns around the table sharing your favorite:

→ song
→ Christmas carol
→ type of music
→ Christian song or hymn

Talk about these Dr. Devo questions.

1. What do you think Jesus thinks of the music kids your age are listening to?

2. What kind of music would Jesus like?

3. What kinds of music and instruments do you think there will be in heaven?

Martin Luther said that music was an outstanding gift of God and that youth should be taught this art, for it makes fine, skillful people. How do you feel about that statement?

Paul wrote:

Let the word of Christ dwell in you richly as you ... sing psalms, hymns, and spiritual songs.

COLOSSIANS 3:16

Music is a wonderful gift from God, and he wants to use it to encourage your faith. So whether on-key or off, sing a joyful song of thanks to the Lord!

Fill in the blank:

Every year more people are killed in Africa by _____ than by lions. Is the answer herons, crocodiles, bees, or bicycles? (I'm waiting for guesses.) The answer is crocodiles. Lions aren't the only dangerous animals in the jungles.

Sometimes the obvious can hurt us. That's how it is with temptation and sin. The Bible tells us:

Be self-controlled and alert. Your enemy the devil prowls around like a roaring lion looking for someone to devour.
1 PETER 5:8

There are times when we know that what we say or do could hurt someone. Some temptations aren't always obvious. Can you think of some examples?

Stay alert. It's a jungle out there. I'm glad Jesus, and not the lion, is the real King of the Jungle. He can lead us away from temptation. He has victory over sin through forgiveness won when he died on the cross and rose on Easter.

Jesus, King of the Jungle, thank you for your forgiveness. Amen.

AN OLD PROBLEM

A boy was visiting his grandmother in a nursing home.

His grandmother's roommate had some peanuts on her desk, and he helped himself. His grandmother said, "I'm so glad you're eating those so they don't go to waste. My roommate doesn't like peanuts. She just sucks the chocolate off them." Ewwwww!

Nursing homes are for people who aren't able to live on their own and need special care. The elderly deserve our respect and attention. Too often we forget what they enjoy and can do. Giving older adults the time, love, and respect they deserve can change their lives and ours.

The Bible says:

> **Gray hair is a crown of splendor.**
> **PROVERBS 16:31**

The elderly are special. They have wisdom and love to offer. They would love to hear how God has affected your life. Not all elderly people believe in Jesus. You can tell them about him. Plan a family visit to a nursing home—even if you don't know anyone there. You and the people you visit will be blessed. (Just don't eat any peanuts!)

A snake crawled over to another snake and asked, "Are we poisonous?"

His friend said, "No, I don't think so."

The first snake responded, "Good! I just bit my lip!"

I love that joke!

Have you bitten your lip lately? It hurts!

It would also be a big problem if we were poisonous like a snake! This may sound silly, but in a way we are poisonous. And we poison ourselves many times a day.

Sin is like a poison. When we make bad choices, we hurt ourselves, and the poison of sin fills us. We can be thankful that God has an answer—an antidote for the poison of sin. His name is Jesus, and he has forgiveness for all our poisonous, hurtful sins.

If we confess our sins, he is faithful and just and will forgive us our sins.

1 JOHN 1:9

PRAYING SCRIPTURE

There is an awesome way to pray for people you may not know too well.

It's called "praying Scripture." It's easy to do! Find a verse from Scripture (the Bible) and add a person's name to it. It makes the Bible and prayer very personal. Below are some examples. Look at the verses and decide who you would like to pray Scripture for, by adding their name to the blank. Then try it and see how it works with some of your other favorite Bible verses.

Protect _____ from the evil one (John 17:15).

Give _____ the strength to obey God, rather than men (Acts 5:29).

May _____ have a pure heart, good conscience, and sincere faith (1 Timothy 1:5).

May _____ love the Lord with all his or her heart, soul, and mind (Matthew 22:37).

May _____ be joyful always, pray continually, and give thanks in all circumstances (1 Thessalonians 5:16–18).

DR. DEVO'S
LICKETY-SPLIT
ROCKET SHOES

TRIPLE PLAY

There are a lot of popular sets of three.

Fill in the blanks:

_____, _____, and I

_____, _____, and spoon

_____, _____, and nothing but the truth

Can you find these other important threes in the Bible?

Here are some clues:

→ gifts of the wise men
→ Jonah and the whale
→ Jesus' crucifixion
→ Peter, after Jesus was arrested

The most important trio isn't really three but one. I'm talking about the triune God. *Tri* means "three," and *une* comes from unity. Three in unity. Three in one. We don't have three Gods but one God. But there are three persons of the triune God. They are the Father, who created us and is the perfect provider and protector; the Son Jesus, who saved the world through his life, death, and resurrection; and the Holy Spirit, who creates faith in us and keeps us in the one true faith.

BUNCHES AND BUNCHES

God's people are often referred to as sheep.

And a bunch of sheep is a flock. Bunches of creatures are referred to by different names. See if you can match the term in the left-hand column with the animals they describe in the right-hand column. (Answers are below.)

1. a colony of_____   a. owls
2. a troop of_____   b. geese
3. a crash of_____   c. rhinoceroses
4. a school of_____   d. ants
5. a gaggle of_____   e. lions
6. a pride of_____   f. fish
7. a parliament of_____   g. monkeys

We are honored to be a part of God's family. Think about some of the different names we are given and what they mean.

→ children of God (1 John 3:1)
→ Jesus' friends (John 15:14)
→ fishers of men (Mark 1:17)
→ branches—Jesus is the Vine (John 15:5)
→ sheep (John 10:1–18)
→ a chosen people, a royal priesthood, a holy nation, a people belonging to God (1 Peter 2:9)

Answers: 1-d, 2-g, 3-c, 4-f, 5-b, 6-e, 7-a.

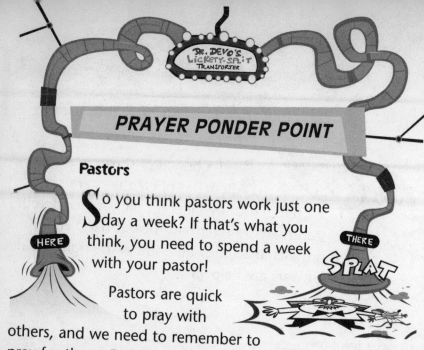

PRAYER PONDER POINT

Pastors

So you think pastors work just one day a week? If that's what you think, you need to spend a week with your pastor!

Pastors are quick to pray with others, and we need to remember to pray for them. Pastors (and their families) deal with so many different and often difficult situations. Here's a starter list for your prayers for pastors.

- wisdom
- insights into God's Word
- personal time with God
- encouragement
- support from congregation
- time for personal interests
- compassion
- family
- joy in serving
- creativity
- leadership gifts

Remember to pray for the pastor in your life. And don't hesitate to let your pastor know you are praying for him or her. You will find that it's a big encouragement to them and a blessing for you as well.

Remember your leaders,
who spoke the word of God to you.
HEBREWS 13:7

THANKS FOR
THE MEMORY

This may sound kind of goofy, but tell your family members who are having devotions with you the following information.

(Go ahead!)

→ your address
→ your phone number
→ the emergency 911 number
→ your birthday and the birth dates of your other family members

As I mentioned, this might seem goofy, but there's a reason for it. These are things that roll right off your tongue. You have committed them to memory because they are vitally important information.

Since that is the case, why do people complain so much about memorizing God's Word? That information is also very important! Isn't it important to have God's promises come to your mind as easily as your phone number? Our minds can handle a lot of information, and knowing God and his Word will save our lives!

Here's a challenge: Each family member is to choose a Bible verse to memorize during the upcoming week. See how you do. Set a date and time to share your verses with each other.

DR. DEVO'S ADVICE COLUMN

Dear Dr. Devo,

I don't know how much you know about what's hot when it comes to fashions, but I am really confused. Tomorrow I'm having my picture taken. I don't know what to wear. I hear that a splash of red looks good in a picture. I want people to notice the red but not my face. What should I wear?

Signed,

Desperate Clotheshorse

Dear Desperate,

You don't need my help for this one. The answer is in the Bible! "What?" you say. "The Bible?" Yes, the answer for your wardrobe problems is in Colossians 3:12: "As God's chosen people, holy and dearly loved, clothe yourselves with compassion, kindness, humility, gentleness and patience."

That should fill your wardrobe with all you need. I can picture you clothed in those outfits!

Clothed in Christ,

Dr. Devo

A DOGGONE GOOD CONVERSATION

If you and your pet would be able to talk to and understand each other for one minute, what would you say to each other? If you don't have any pets, what about a conversation with your computer, your favorite character from a book, the walls of your room? I'd love to hear all your answers! There will be some doggone hilarious ones, I'm sure!

If you could talk to someone in the Bible right now (besides God or Jesus) for one minute, who would it be and what would you say to each other?

If you could talk to Jesus right now for one minute about what is on your mind this very second, what would you say? How do you think he would respond?

If you could talk to Jesus right now—hey, doggone it! What are you waiting for? Take that minute. Have that talk. Listen for answers.

Dear friends, build yourselves up in your
most holy faith and pray in the Holy Spirit.

JUDE 20

Connect the dots for a big surprise!

Go ahead! What's the matter? I guess it's pretty obvious, huh?

That heart reminds me of something that may seem obvious—but be glad that it is! In fact, you've heard it many times through these devotions. But I hope you never grow tired of hearing it or knowing it. Here's the news:

Jesus loves you.

It may be obvious but it's the most important truth in your world.

Jesus—you. Jesus—faith. Jesus—love. Jesus—forgiveness. Jesus—happiness. Jesus—heaven. Get the connection? Everything is connected to Jesus.

THE EYES HAVE IT

Get some paper and a pen or pencil.

Take turns drawing the objects listed below. Oh, there's one other rule. The drawings must be done with your eyes closed! Go for it!

→ a snowman
→ a fancy crown
→ a tree with a swing

It's not very easy, is it? Sight is a great gift from God. But the Bible also says:

We live by faith, not by sight.
2 CORINTHIANS 5:7

Even more important than our eyesight is God's gift of faith. Having good eyesight won't get anyone into heaven. But God's gift of faith in Jesus as our personal Savior opens heaven's door. Good eyes of faith are needed to live a life pleasing to God in his world. The things we see around us can lead us away from him. When we live by faith—by totally trusting in God in all things—we begin to see what real living is all about! One day you can look him in the eyes and thank him in person!

FACE-OFF

Human beings are selfish by nature.

It's easy to get into the habit of looking at ourselves in the mirror and thinking we are the center of the universe. The most commonly used word in English conversation is *I*. We like to talk about ourselves! We want things to go our way. We want to be noticed.

Paul warned us about this when he wrote:

There will be terrible times in the last days. People will be lovers of themselves, lovers of money, boastful, proud, abusive, disobedient to their parents, ungrateful, unholy, without love.

2 TIMOTHY 3:1–3

Lord, let there be more of you in our lives and less of us. Forgive us. Give us strength in these selfish times. In Jesus' name we pray. Amen.

WHAT WILL YOU BE REMEMBERED FOR?

Even people who are not baseball fans have probably heard of Babe Ruth.

He was one of the greatest home run hitters ever. That's what he is known for. Since we're talking baseball, do you know who holds the world record for most career strikeouts? Give up? Babe Ruth! Most people only know the slugger for the great number of homers he hit. But there were many times he failed to even hit the ball. Strike one. Strike two. Strike three. You're out, Babe.

I guess none of us want to be remembered for our failures. That's why it is such great news that although God takes our sins very seriously, he also offers us forgiveness. The sacrifice of Jesus on the cross covers all our sins—past, present, and future ones. And when we are forgiven, we have an opportunity to begin again and live our lives in ways that will be remembered for good. We have an awesome God!

One day when my oldest son was about six years old and playing in the yard, he called out, "Mommy, this worm is sticking his tongue out at me!" She quickly found him eye to eye with a little snake that was indeed sticking out its tongue!

A worm with a tongue is as unheard of as a snake with ears. Since snakes don't have ears, God gave them a tongue that is very sensitive to the vibrations sounds make. By flicking its tongue, a snake picks up the sound waves and "hears" in this special way.

Snakes have an excuse for not hearing. We don't! Sometimes we are so focused on ourselves that we don't respect what others are saying by listening to them. It's also easy not to listen to God speaking to us through the life and words of Jesus. A good excuse for not listening to God is unheard of.

"Hear" what God says in John 5:24; Romans 10:17; James 1:22–26.

PICTURE THIS

One of the most popular paintings is the Mona Lisa by Leonardo da Vinci.

You probably know what it looks like. Here are some things you may not know about the painting.

➡ Mona has no eyebrows because it was the latest thing during that time in Italy for women to shave them off!

➡ The painting is pretty small—twenty-one inches by thirty inches.

➡ According to one report, X-rays of the picture show that Leonardo painted three different versions under the final portrait.

I, Dr. Devo, think there are a few things to learn from this.

Shaving your eyebrows was "in" during the 1500s, but don't try it today!

Even if you're not all that big or if you are very big—you're still a masterpiece!

Unlike Mona Lisa, God created you only once, and you were perfect the first time. He never wishes he had created you differently. He has blessed you with just the right gifts and talents to be a picture of success!

YOU'RE GETTING ON MY NERVES

How many nerves do you think there are in the human body?

Here are three choices:

→ 36 feet
→ 124 feet
→ 45 miles

Don't get nervous when I tell you that the human body has forty-five miles of nerves! If you don't believe me, all I can say is, "You've got a lot of nerve!"

Because in general we are different, selfish, obnoxious at times, hurtful, sometimes mean, and all around sinful, it is absolutely 110 percent certain that we will get on each other's nerves quite often. But we should each want to take our forty-five miles of nerves and work together for miles of smiles.

Paul had it right when he wrote:

Put up with each other. Forgive the things you are holding against one another. Forgive, just as the Lord forgave you.... Let the peace that Christ gives rule in your hearts. As parts of one body, you were appointed to live in peace. And be thankful.

COLOSSIANS 3:13, 15 NIrV

THE COFFIN PROBLEM

Some people are fearful of death, dying, and even going to a funeral home.

At funerals in ancient China, when the lid of a coffin was closed, people would step back so their shadows wouldn't get caught in the box. But God doesn't want us to live in fear of death.

Through Jesus, God provided medicine to stop the "coffin problem." Jesus died. His body was put in a tomb. But then he rose from the dead. Jesus lives! He lives forever and for us!

Paul used two Old Testament verses to share the good news about death for believers:

Death has been swallowed up. It has lost the battle.... Death, where is the battle you thought you were winning? Death, where is your sting?

1 CORINTHIANS 15:54-55 NIrV

That's great "medicine" when funerals make us sad. Jesus won the battle with death. We will be together forever in heaven with our family and friends who die believing in Jesus.

Which family member do you think used the most words today?

Approximately how many words do you think the average American knows? Here are some choices.

- **a.** one thousand words
- **b.** five thousand words
- **c.** ten thousand words
- **d.** one million words

The answer—I'll whisper it so no one else can hear—is c.

That's a lot of words! What's more important than knowing a lot of words is knowing how to use them. How many of the ten thousand words the average person uses could be called unwholesome, which means "evil" or "bad"? Unfortunately, all of our words aren't used in the best way.

Listen to these wholesome words:

Do not let any unwholesome talk come out of your mouths, but only what is helpful for building others up according to their needs, that it may benefit those who listen.
    EPHESIANS 4:29

Now think of ways you can use your words to encourage and help people instead of speaking in an unwholesome way. Then use wholesome words as you pray to our holy God.

46

IS THERE HAM IN HAMBURGER?

I've always wondered how hamburger got its name.

The "burger" part isn't what bothers me. It's the "ham" part. There isn't any ham in hamburgers!

Now, I know there aren't any pans in pancakes, but they are little cakes made in pans. So that makes sense!

Another one of those words is *Christian.* Is Christ in a Christian? Let's think about that. People watch what we do and listen to what we say. I doubt if all of them are thinking, *It's obvious that person is a Christian!* We want people to "see" Christ living in us as we play, worship, write, talk on the phone, do things on the computer, and in every way that we live. We have been given Christ's name. We are Christians. Through God's love, forgiveness, and life we learn how to proudly wear his name and strive to live like him.

From the Father his whole family in heaven and on earth gets its name.... Christ will live in your hearts because you believe in him.

EPHESIANS 3:15, 17 NIrV

There are some of you reading this who haven't learned about angles in math yet.

To learn about angles, let's use a Dr. Devo family volunteer. (Pick someone!)

Have the person stand up and face the dirty spot on the window. (I bet there's a spot!) With the help of someone who knows about angles, have that person turn 90 degrees. Next, have them turn 180 degrees from their original position. And finally, have them turn 360 degrees from where they started. They should now be facing the same dirty spot on the window.

Angles can teach about repentance. When we have sinned, we are following Satan's way. We have turned 180 degrees, with our backs to God. When we repent, it is like we are making another 180-degree turn. The Holy Spirit leads us to turn completely around until our backs are to our sin, being truly sorry and facing the opposite direction—toward the will of our forgiving Savior. That's the life-changing angle on repentance!

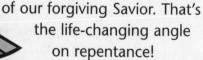

DR. DEVO'S
ADVICE COLUMN

Dear Dr. Devo,

I'm sick and tired of school. I'm never going to use this stuff I'm supposed to be learning. But if I don't do my homework, my parents and my teachers get upset with me.

Signed,

Bored with School

P.S. I do like recess.

Dear Bored with School,

You think it's bad when your parents and teachers correct you? How would you feel if God had something to say to you about this, too? He does! "Anyone who loves to be trained loves knowledge. Anyone who hates to be corrected is stupid" (Proverbs 12:1 NIrV).

How's that for a zinger? I know you won't need to know everything you learn in school, but you don't know what will help and what won't. Education is very important. God has blessed you with a good brain and a good body! I'll pray that you start to look at your education in a better light. You might try praying for that, too!

May God bring out his best in you,

Dr. Devo

49

SHELLING OUT THE TRUTH

Have you held a big seashell to your ear to hear the ocean?

That's cool, isn't it? Well, I hate to burst your bubble, but that sound isn't the ocean you're hearing. It's just an echo of the blood pulsing in your ear! That kind of ruins the fun, doesn't it? That's okay; I just tell myself that it's the ocean so I can enjoy it.

Paul and Timothy were pastors who probably listened to a few seashells. But they spent most of their time telling people the truth about the world's Savior. The truth is that people are sinners and sinners need a Savior. Jesus is that Savior! And all who trust in Jesus as their Savior, as the Bible says, will receive the gift of heaven. That's the truth.

But Paul warned Timothy about some things. He wrote:

The time will come when people won't put up with true teachings....
They will gather a large number of teachers around them.
The teachers will say what the people want to hear.

2 TIMOTHY 4:3 NIrV

I know the truth about seashells yet I want to believe it's the ocean I hear. But when it comes to believing the Bible, we can't pick and choose what we want to believe. The entire Bible is the true Word of God!

THE FRUIT CALLED LOVE

The fruit of the Spirit is love, joy, peace, patience, kindness, goodness, faithfulness, gentleness and self-control.

GALATIANS 5:22-23

Foreign language lesson for the day: The Greek word for love in Galatians 5:22 is *agape* (pronounced "ah-gahp-*ay*"). Agape is the way God loves. It's a selfless (not selfish), protective, always caring, gentle, thoughtful, perfect kind of love. And that's how God wants us to love him and others. We won't be able to love perfectly until we get to heaven, but that's the goal he has for us. Can you imagine if everyone in the world loved with an agape kind of love?

Use the letters below (which spell out "agape love") to think of words that describe how God loves you.

a _____

g _____

a _____

p _____

e _____

l _____

o _____

v _____

e _____

THE FRUIT CALLED JOY

The fruit of the Spirit is love, joy, peace, patience, kindness, goodness, faithfulness, gentleness and self-control.

GALATIANS 5:22-23

I have a friend whose name is Joy but I don't think she's always joyful about it. She says people who meet her are always making some comment about the word *joy*. Sometimes they even start singing songs about *joy*. Stop for a minute. How many songs (don't forget the Christmas songs) can your family think of that have the word joy in them? There are quite a few.

Joy is a great word—short, happy, fun! Joy! Joy! Joy! Say it out loud! Sing the word! Enjoy the word!

The amazing word *joy* describes the kind of life God wants for us—joyful! Do you have the joy, joy, joy, joy down in your heart? Hey, that's a joy song! Let the Spirit in and place his gift of joy even into the corners of your life that don't seem to be joyful!

THE FRUIT CALLED PEACE

The fruit of the Spirit is love, joy, peace, patience, kindness, goodness, faithfulness, gentleness and self-control.

GALATIANS 5:22–23

My family loves fruit. Well, all of them but me. So every once in a while I'll have a piece of fruit, and they all make a big deal out of it. God makes a big deal out of a piece of spiritual fruit called *peace*.

God's peace is different from any other kind of peace we can find in this world. It isn't like sacking out on the couch and watching TV. God can calm us down when we are nervous about a test or need to have confidence when a bully is around us. He gives us peace to face our struggles and come out a winner.

Think of a peaceful word and play a game of hangman with your family. Give the hangman a look that isn't peaceful. Remember the peaceful word that is below him and give God thanks for the peace he has given you in Jesus.

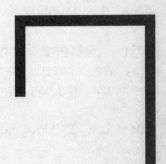

THE FRUIT CALLED PATIENCE

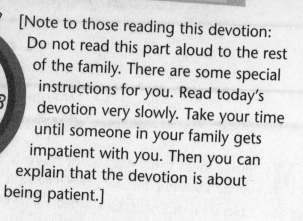

[Note to those reading this devotion: Do not read this part aloud to the rest of the family. There are some special instructions for you. Read today's devotion very slowly. Take your time until someone in your family gets impatient with you. Then you can explain that the devotion is about being patient.]

The fruit of the Spirit is love, joy, peace, patience, kindness, goodness, faithfulness, gentleness and self-control.

GALATIANS 5:22-23

Question 1: When is it tough for you to be patient? (Wait for answers. And no, this isn't a joke!)

Question 2: Are you finding it difficult to be patient listening to this devotion read slowly?

Being patient is hard! One of the reasons is that we always want things to go our way. And we want things to go according to our timing.

Question 3: How can we become more patient?

Answer: Realize it's a gift for you from the Holy Spirit. Receive it freely and joyfully! Learn from God, thanking him for his patience with you.

THE FRUIT CALLED KINDNESS

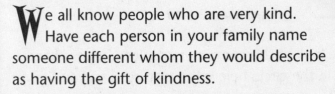

The fruit of the Spirit is love, joy, peace, patience, kindness, goodness, faithfulness, gentleness and self-control.

GALATIANS 5:22–23

We all know people who are very kind. Have each person in your family name someone different whom they would describe as having the gift of kindness.

Answer these questions about that person.

→ Have they been a kind person as long as you've known them?
→ What makes the difference between this person and others?
→ Does this person have a strong faith in Jesus Christ?
→ What can you learn from this person about kindness?

Put together a special prayer list for your kind friends and relations. Close the prayer by giving thanks for each family member and the kindness they show.

1. _____
2. _____
3. _____
4. _____
5. _____
6. _____

THE FRUIT CALLED GOODNESS

The fruit of the Spirit is love, joy, peace,
patience, kindness, goodness, faithfulness,
gentleness and self-control.

GALATIANS 5:22–23

Take a close look at the computer art piece below. Place your nose in the circle below the picture. Can you figure out what it is?

```
            #####^^^^^^^^^^^^^^^^^//////####
           !@#$!@#$!@#$!@#$!@#$!@#$!@#$!@#$
           $$$$$$$$$$$$$$$####$$$$$$$####$$$$$$$$$$
*****$$$$$###*****@@@@@\\\\\\\\
           %^&*%^&*%^&*%^&*%^&*%^&*%^&*%^&*%^&*
           ||||||||||||||||^^^^^^^^^^^^||||||||||||||
```

Goodness is one of the fruits of God's Spirit. We would like to believe that everyone is basically good. Actually, everyone is sinful. That means we don't act very good sometimes. Goodness may seem like an odd gift to pray for and enjoy, but it's an important part of our forgiven life in Jesus Christ.

Oh, by the way, I wanted to show you how easy it is to act badly. There is no picture in the symbols above. I thought you might like to feel foolish by putting the book up to your nose. Oh, for goodness' sake, that was bad of me!

THE FRUIT CALLED FAITHFULNESS

The fruit of the Spirit is love, joy, peace,
patience, kindness, goodness, faithfulness,
gentleness and self-control.

GALATIANS 5:22-23

Do you still count on your fingers? I do. Every day. It's true. I count on my fingers to type on the keys of the computer. I count on them to be able to hold books. I count on them to grip a pen, cup, fork, and many other things.

You probably thought I was talking about using your fingers for adding or subtracting. (Gotcha!) But I wanted to remind you that it's important for you to be someone that people can count on when you give your word. That's called faithfulness.

God wants us to be faithful to him and others. When we make a promise or a commitment, we should keep it, just as God is faithful to keep all of his promises. To learn more about faithfulness, read and talk about Psalm 100 and 117.

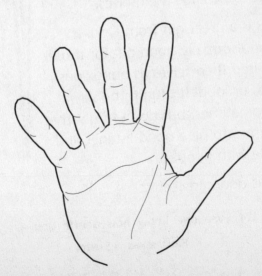

The fruit of the Spirit is love, joy, peace, patience, kindness, goodness, faithfulness, gentleness and self-control.

GALATIANS 5:22–23

Which of these words best describes you? (Have each family member do this about themselves.)

happy	calm
patient	honest
loud	wild
hyper	fun
gentle	sweet
obnoxious	faithful

When someone picked a word that described them, I would guess that not everyone agreed. I'm also guessing that no one in your family used the word *gentle* to describe themselves.

Gentleness is a great gift from God. It could be an especially good gift for those who described themselves as obnoxious, hyper, wild, or loud! It's fun to be silly and loud sometimes, but don't forget that there are times to be a good listener and to be gentle with people.

Paul has this good advice:

Let everyone know how gentle you are.

PHILIPPIANS 4:5 NIrV

THE FRUIT CALLED SELF-CONTROL

The fruit of the Spirit is love, joy, peace, patience, kindness, goodness, faithfulness, gentleness and self-control.

GALATIANS 5:22-23

Self-control is easy to describe. If you are reading this at mealtime, look at the leftover food around you. What if I gave you permission to put one of those veggies on your fork and sling it across the room at someone in your family? Would you do it? What about an all-out food fight?

You guys are itching to try this now, aren't you? I planted a wild and crazy idea in your head and you want to go for it. Please—control yourself!

I'm sure you have weapons (forks and spoons) along with ammunition (food) every night, but you don't have daily food fights. You could but you don't. You exercise self-control. Thank the Holy Spirit for his gift of self-control in your life and home! And for times when you need help with self-control, ask for help, strength, and forgiveness.

Lord, today show me how to exercise self-control in everything I do. Amen.

TWISTERS!

Tongue twisters can be lots of fun.

Here's one you might like: I thought a thought. But the thought I thought wasn't the thought I thought I thought.

Here's another: Suddenly swerving, seven small swans swam silently southward, seeing six swift sailboats.

And finally:

> I do not understand what I do. For what I want
> to do I do not do, but what I hate I do....
> For what I do is not the good I want to do;
> no, the evil I do not want to do—
> this I keep on doing.

Now here's another twist: the last tongue twister is from the Bible. Paul wrote it in Romans 7:15, 19. Paul was struggling between what he wanted to do and what he did. We've all done that. We know what God wants us to do but so often we do just the opposite. When temptation and sin twist our lives up, the only way to get unraveled is to turn to Jesus for help. He's the answer to our struggles.

PRAYER PONDER POINT

Prayer in Schools

Question: Why should fish be very smart creatures?

Answer: They spend so much time in schools!

Even if the government says students can't have public prayers in public schools, you need to pray for schools and teachers! You can probably think of a lot of specific people and things to pray for on that topic. Make your own additions to this prayer list:

- janitors
- teachers
- bullies
- bus drivers
- secretaries
- volunteers
- principals
- librarians
- Christian teachers
- substitute teachers
- school boards
- cafeteria workers

You spend a lot of time in school. And schools all over the world would be different if people spent as much time praying for schools as kids spent in them.
Be a student of prayer! Learn to trust in God, who answers prayers!

He answered their prayers, because they trusted in him.
1 CHRONICLES 5:20

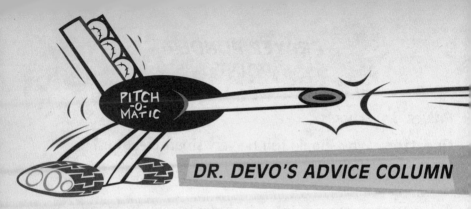

DR. DEVO'S ADVICE COLUMN

Dear Dr. Devo,

I am bad about interrupting people before they're finished talking. I don't listen to what they have to say, and I—

Dear Interrupter,

It is rude to interrupt someone. Oops, I didn't let you finish.

Signed,

Dr. Devo

Dear Dr. Devo,

That's all I had to say. My parents say it's rude to interrupt. They want me to respect what others are saying. What do you think?

Signed,

Preteen Interrupter

Dear Preteen Interrupter,

Here's what God has to say. Let's all listen without interruption. "To answer before listening is foolish and shameful" (Proverbs 18:13 NIrv).

No more needs to be said!

Dr. Devo

IT'S MEANINGLESS . . . ISN'T IT?

Whatever!

Big deal! Who cares! So what? Who gives a rip? What's the point? This is lame!

Bet you've said those words once or twice when you thought something was dumb or meaningless.

The book of Ecclesiastes in the Bible is all about life being meaningless. *Ecclesiastes* means "teacher." For twelve chapters "the Teacher" talks about how everything in life is lame. What's the point? Whatever! Who gives a rip? But at the end of the book, we find out that his point is to teach us that everything in life will seem meaningless unless God is a part of it.

After the griping and complaining, the Teacher finally ends by writing:

> Everything has now been heard. And here's the final thing I want to say. Have respect for God and obey his commandments. That's what every being should do.
>
> ECCLESIASTES 12:13 NIrV

Sounds like a meaningful plan to me! What do you think?

CROSS BETWEENS

Question 1: What do you get if you cross an owl with a skunk?

Answer: A bird that smells but doesn't give a hoot!

Question 2: What do you get if you cross a tiger with a snowman?

Answer: Frostbite!

Question 3: Have you ever seen a cross between earth and heaven?

Answer: Now you have: earth + heaven

earth ———— *heaven above*

Jesus' death on the cross is the only way to heaven from earth. Because Jesus died and rose from the dead for us, all who believe in him can have eternal life in heaven. Jesus said:

I am the way and the truth and the life.
No one comes to the Father except through me.
JOHN 14:6

We need to get this news out to everyone—those across the street, across town, across the country, and across the world!

LEARNING A "RIDDLE" BIT ABOUT GOD'S WORD

Here's a tough riddle:

Begin with the word *snowing* and take one letter away to form another word. Keep taking one letter away to form another word until you end up with a one-letter word. Cover the bottom of this page if you don't want to see the answers.

six-letter word: _ _ _ _ _ _

five-letter word: _ _ _ _ _

four-letter word: _ _ _ _

three-letter word: _ _ _

two-letter word: _ _

one-letter word: _

The remaining words show how our Christian lives start breaking down, like the riddle. We start with clean, white snow (Isaiah 1:18). Knowing we are forgiven, we love telling others about God's love by *sowing* (James 3:18). *Swing*ing and *sing*ing are examples of joyful living (Nehemiah 8:10; Psalm 147:1). But then look at the last three words: *sin, in, I*. We see how sin is within us (1 John 1:8). That leads us right back to checking out God's forgiveness story in Isaiah 1:18 again.

Answers: *sowing, swing, sing, sin, in, I*

Dr. Devo's riddle time!

This is a toughie: Name an English word that begins and ends with the letters *he* (in that order). There are two possible answers but he-he isn't one of them! (Ha-ha! Nice try!)

Clue 1: One is eight letters long; the other is nine.

Clue 2: The third to the last letter in each word is c.

Clue 3: Each word includes a body part.

Clue 4: This verse might give you an idea for the answer:

He heals the brokenhearted and binds up their wounds.
PSALM 147:3

READY FOR THE ANSWERS? Headache AND heartache.

This riddle focused around the word *he.* So does Psalm 147. The focus is on the one who gets all the praise and worship from the one who wrote the psalm. "He" is the Lord. He heals the brokenhearted (those with heartaches) and binds up their wounds (even headaches).

The Lord can bring us hope, help, and even joy. He heals us through his life and love. He is the beginning and the end of all we need.

WHAT DO YOU GET WITH A CROSS?

Question 1: What do you get if you cross a cocker spaniel, a poodle, and a rooster?

Answer: A cockerpoodledoo!

Question 2: What do you get if you cross a rooster, a disciple, and a look?

Answer: A guilty conscience.

Okay, the second riddle isn't funny but it is true! Read Luke 22:33–34, 54–62. (Go ahead! I'll wait.) Do you remember this?

→ The rooster crowed.
→ The disciple Peter, remembered what Jesus had told him earlier about denying him.
→ Peter realized he had denied Jesus.
→ Jesus looked straight at Peter.
→ The look caused Peter to feel guilty.

God sends us reminders throughout our day about how to live as Jesus' disciple. He also sends us reminders when we fail. Maybe it's a look from a parent, a Bible verse, words from a teacher or friend, or even a cross. The cross reminds us of our sins and even our Savior, who can wipe away our guilt. That's what you get when you cross Jesus and a guilty sinner. Forgiveness!

Noah was an *ark*itect who trusted God and his Word. What the Lord told him, Noah did (read Genesis 6:9, 22). The animals did the same thing. They came to Noah by God's leading. There was Mr. Deer and his dear deer wife, Doe. The kangaroos came on a leap of faith, hopping to find safety from the upcoming flood. When they met Noah, they knew they had not jumped to the wrong conclusion about God's will for their lives. The elephants would need king-sized beds and an extra large room to place their trunks. The owls wouldn't give a hoot where they stayed.

As always, God kept his promise. It rained cats and dogs for forty days and nights. (That's 960 hours or 57,600 minutes of rain!) Noah and his family trusted God through thunder, lightning, and the elephant's snoring.

The great lesson for Noah (and us) is that God reigns over his world and pours out blessings, flooding creation with love.

The Lord reigns, he is robed in majesty.

Psalm 93:1

DON'T FORGET TO REMEMBER

Get a reading partner for this devotion. One reads character 1 and the other, character 2.

Character 1: Would you remember me in a month?

Character 2: Sure!

Character 1: Would you remember me in a week?

Character 2: Of course.

Character 1: Would you remember me in a day?

Character 2: I'll remember.

Character 1: Would you remember me in an hour?

Character 2: Sure!

Character 1: Knock, knock.

Character 2: Who's there?

Character 1: You forgot me already!

Did you forget God today? What caused him to come to mind? Why does it seem easy to forget his promises and love and trust ourselves instead? What can you do so you won't forget to remember him? Thankfully, he'll never forget us or our need for him!

Remember your Creator in the days of your youth.

ECCLESIASTES 12:1

Knock, knock

Who's there?

Cargo!

Cargo who?

Cargo beep, beep.

Knock, knock

Who's there?

Duey

Duey who?

Duey have to keep telling knock-knock jokes?

Duey have to go to church? Duey have to go to Sunday school? Duey have to have family devotions? Duey have to pray together? Duey? Duey? Duey?

Take a look at how the Bible answers those questions:

Let us not give up meeting together. Some are in the habit of doing this. Instead, let us cheer each other up with words of hope. Let us do it all the more as you see the day coming when Christ will return.

HEBREWS 10:25 NIrV

WHAT DO YOU CALL A MAN?

Question 1: What do you call a man with some cat scratches on his head?

Answer: Claude!

Question 2: What do you call a man that doesn't sink?

Answer: Bob!

Question 3: What do you call a man who is one hundred percent man and one hundred percent God?

Answer: Jesus Christ!

Jesus is true man and true God. We know he was born of a woman, Mary, as a true human being. He was thirsty, tired, and he felt pain. But he was also true God. Jesus said:

> **1 and the Father are one.**
>
> **JOHN 10:30**

He knew all things, did miracles, forgave sins, was all-powerful and more.

Even though he is true God, he didn't flaunt his "Godness" here on the earth. He wanted and needed to feel and experience the things we do. He even had to face suffering and death for us as a human and keep God's law perfectly because we couldn't.

Man, oh man, what a great God we have!

Do brooms grow on trees?

It sounds like they do according to the Bible. Check this out:

> Elijah was afraid and ran for his life.... He came to a broom tree, sat down under it and prayed that he might die. "I have had enough, LORD," he said.... Then he lay down under the tree and fell asleep.
>
> 1 KINGS 19:3-5

A broom tree is a desert bush, not a tree where brooms grow. But what's important is if you have ever had feelings like Elijah! If so, please talk about it with your parents or another adult you trust. It's a terrible feeling being so sad that it seems like no one cares or can help.

An angel of the Lord brought food and drink to Elijah. And God provided strength, hope, and love so he was able to carry on. God has those same gifts for you. I hope you have broom for that sweet, sweep news in your life!

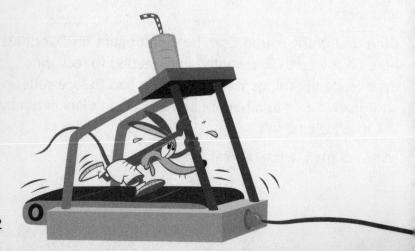

LET GOD IN THE DRIVER'S SEAT

Question 1: What kind of vehicle does Mickey Mouse's girlfriend drive?

Answer: A Minnie van!

Question 2: What does God drive?

Answer: Enemies out of the area!

God promised his people he had a land picked out for them. But before God's people arrived in the Promised Land, they had to get past the unbelieving people who lived there. Remember that when God made a promise, he kept it—whatever it took! Sometimes he sent an angel (not a Minnie van) to drive out the enemies! Check this out:

> I am sending an angel ahead of you. He will guard you along the way. He will bring you to the place I have prepared.... I will drive them out ahead of you little by little. I will do it until your numbers have increased enough for you to take control of the land.
>
> EXODUS 23:20, 30 NIrV

As you travel to the Promised Land of heaven, God needs to be in the driver's seat! Enjoy the ride, remembering that God still keeps his promises!

SHEDDING SOME LIGHT ON JESUS

Question: What did the little lightbulb say to his father?

Answer: I wuv you watts and watts!

Jesus said:

> I am the light of the world. Whoever follows me will never walk in darkness, but will have the light of life.
>
> JOHN 8:12

Jesus also said:

> You are the light of the world.
>
> MATTHEW 5:14

(Now you can tell everyone truthfully that you are a very bright person! Jesus says so!)

Jesus says he is the light of the world. He also says *we* are the light of the world. How can that be? What does he mean when he talks about never walking in the dark? Can you be a light to the world this week? How has Jesus been a light in the darkness of your life?

Dear Light of the World, we love you watts and watts. Thanks for bringing light to the darkness of our lives. Use us as lights in your world as we reflect your perfect light. Amen.

BEAUTY-FULL

Question: Why are *a*, *e*, and *u* the prettiest vowels?

Answer: Because you can't have beauty without them.

Here's a verse from the Bible about beauty:

> Your beauty should not come from outward adornment,
> such as braided hair and the wearing of gold jewelry and
> fine clothes. Instead, it should be that of your inner self,
> the unfading beauty of a gentle and quiet spirit,
> which is of great worth in God's sight.
>
> 1 PETER 3:3-4

Maybe you've heard that beauty comes from the inside. Outward looks can't compare with being thoughtful, kind, and encouraging. Spend more time being beautiful or handsome in this way.

God is filled with beauty. Talk with your family about God's beauty. Close by reading the verse below, praying the words of the psalm writer.

> I'm asking the LORD for only one thing. Here is what I want. I want to live in the house of the LORD all the days of my life. I want to look at the beauty of the LORD. I want to worship him in his temple.
>
> PSALM 27:4 NIrV

I found this great translation of 1 Corinthians 13:4–7 called "Love Passage for Kids" in *The Adventure Bible for Young Readers* by Zonderkidz. It describes God's perfect love for us. It also reminds us of how we are to love others, patterning our relationships after the way he loves us.

Love will stand in line and wait its turn.

Love looks for the good in others.

Love doesn't always want what others have, and it doesn't brag about what it does have.

Love is polite, even when the other person is rude.

Love doesn't always have to be first.

Love doesn't get angry over the small things, and it doesn't remember one reason after another to be hurt.

Love isn't happy when someone else fails, but is happy with the truth.

Love will always protect others, especially those who are often picked on or teased.

Love always believes the best about others and is steady and true.

You might want to read this another time or two to let it sink in and affect your loving heart.

FRIENDS

A friend loves at all times.
PROVERBS 17:17

True Christian friends are great gifts from heaven. After answering some friendly questions with your family, use the word *friendship* below to explain what you think a friend is. Using each letter, write a word that describes a really good friend.

Why is your best friend your best friend? What do you like most about your friends? Would God approve of your friends? Would your friends care about you even when you're in a bad situation? When is the last time you told your friends how much you appreciate them? Are you a good friend to others?

f _____

r _____

i _____

e _____

n _____

d _____

s _____

h _____

i _____

p _____

Traveling Prayers

As you travel, spend some time praying as a family or by yourself. Here's one idea you could use. Think about ten different groups to pray for. Then pray for that number of persons within the group. For instance, pray for one principal, two family members, three neighbors, four friends, five unbelievers, six teachers, etc. Be creative and passionate as you pray!

Take time to pray for those who are traveling right now. Some drivers on long trips may be tired—pray that they receive extra energy or find a place to pull over and rest. Pray for truck drivers as well as police patrolling the roads. Thank God for seat belts, air bags, and other safety devices. What are other traveling prayers you can think of?

The apostle Paul was a traveler who wrote:

> I serve God with my whole heart. I preach the good news about his Son. God knows that I always remember you in my prayers. I pray that now at last it may be God's plan to open the way for me to visit you.
>
> ROMANS 1:9-10 NIrV

Dear Dr. Devo,

I was elected president of our class. I've had this job for a few months now and I'm getting really tired of doing everything. I thought this was going to be easy! There's so much to do. I feel like I'm doing it all by myself. I shouldn't complain. I feel better already. I can handle things by myself. Thanks for listening!

Signed,

Miss President

Dear Miss President,

Being a leader can be lonely at times. I doubt if you have as many kids in your class as Moses had to lead out of Egypt! He had about two million! He was trying to do all the work, too. Then his father-in-law, Jethro (yes, his name was Jethro), told him about a better way to be a leader. Jethro told Moses to get others to help. You can't handle all the work by yourself. I'd encourage you to read Exodus 18:13–27 so you can become the kind of leader God wants you to be.

Humbly,

Dr. Devo

When Jesus was tempted by Satan, he fought back with a verse from the Old Testament. Knowing God's Word is very important. In the next few devotions, we're going to get to know the Bible a little better. By learning the books of the Bible, there will be more joy in studying God's Word.

Here's a tip on remembering the number of books in the Bible: How many letters are in the word *old?* (Three.) How many letters in *testament?* (Nine.) Put the three and the nine next to each other and you have thirty-nine. There are thirty-nine books in the Old Testament.

The New Testament starts with Jesus' birth and life and tells of the beginning of the Christian church. There are also three letters in the word *new,* and *testament* still has nine letters. Multiply three times nine and you get twenty-seven. There are twenty-seven books in the New Testament.

Here's some other new math you can use when Satan tempts you, like he tempted Jesus:
3 nails + 1 Savior = 4giveness.

LEARNING THE BOOKS— THE FIRST FIVE

The first five books of the Bible have some special names:

Torah, Pentateuch (meaning "five books"), or the Books of Moses. They are:

➡ *Genesis* (meaning "beginning") tells how God created the world and introduces us to some faithful people like Adam, Eve, Noah, Abraham, Sarah, Isaac, Jacob, Joseph, and others.

➡ *Exodus* (meaning "leaving") tells how God led his people out of their imprisonment in Egypt after 430 years and toward the land of Canaan, which he had promised to them.

➡ *Leviticus* is a book about the rules of the Levites, which were the religious leaders. (It shows how God is teaching the people to trust him.)

➡ *Numbers* gets its name because it starts with a census (a count) of the Israelites in the wilderness as they are being led to the Promised Land. It talks about their trip and God's faithfulness.

➡ *Deuteronomy* (meaning "repeating the law") is a kind of summary book of the last three.

Now say the names of the books together three times!

Remember what God says:

Fix these words of mine in your hearts and minds.

DEUTERONOMY 11:18

LEARNING THE BOOKS— JOSHUA TO ESTHER

The next twelve books of the Bible tell the history of God's people. That's why they are often called historical books! (Who would have thunk it?) Some great stories of God's people like Joshua, Ruth, Samson, Deborah, Samuel, Saul, David, Jonathan, and Solomon are told here. You'll also find stories of God's grace (undeserved love) in many of the lives of the kings, along with the temple builders, the temple rebuilders, and beautiful queen Esther.

This passage tells us why we want to learn God's Word:

> As for God, his way is perfect; the word of the LORD is flawless. He is a shield for all who take refuge in him.
>
> **2 SAMUEL 22:31**

Take some time to learn these twelve historical books, letting "his story" into your heart.

- ➡ Joshua
- ➡ Judges
- ➡ Ruth
- ➡ 1 Samuel
- ➡ 2 Samuel
- ➡ 1 Kings
- ➡ 2 Kings
- ➡ 1 Chronicles
- ➡ 2 Chronicles
- ➡ Ezra
- ➡ Nehemiah
- ➡ Esther

LEARNING THE BOOKS—
POETRY AND WISDOM

Question 1: What do you get when you cross an octopus and a cow?

Answer: A cow that can milk herself!

Question 2: What do you get when you cross poetry and wisdom?

Answer: The next five books of the Bible!

➡ *Job* tells the story of a man who trusted God, even when he lost everything in his life—family, work, and land.

➡ *Psalms* are songs and prayers. This was the songbook for God's people. Different people wrote them. Some are words of praise; others are sad. There are 150 psalms.

➡ *Proverbs* are wise sayings. Solomon wrote many of them. He was the wisest man ever.

➡ *Ecclesiastes* is also a book of wisdom. Probably written by Solomon, the book's message is that everything is meaningless without God.

➡ *Song of Songs* is a poetic love story. It tells us that God loves us and wants us to know him.

Add the poetry and wisdom books to your list and try to say them from memory!

LEARNING THE BOOKS—
THE PROPHETS

Here's a challenge for you: memorizing the books of the prophets. The prophets were ministers of God, who lived during the times of the great kings of Israel. God used them to warn the people about their sin and to give them hope by revealing that God would send a Savior to liberate them.

There are seventeen books of the prophets in all. Based on their length, the first four (excluding Lamentations) are called the Major Prophets and the rest are called the Minor Prophets. These are the books of the prophets.

➡ Isaiah
➡ Jeremiah
➡ Lamentations (of Jeremiah)
➡ Ezekiel
➡ Daniel
➡ Hosea
➡ Joel
➡ Amos
➡ Obadiah

➡ Jonah
➡ Micah
➡ Nahum
➡ Habakkuk
➡ Zephaniah
➡ Haggai
➡ Zechariah
➡ Malachi

My word ... will not return to me empty, but will accomplish what I desire and achieve the purpose for which I sent it.

ISAIAH 55:11

LEARNING THE BOOKS—
HEADING INTO THE NEW TESTAMENT

A little boy wrote this letter in Sunday school:

"**D**ear God, we had a good time at church today. Wish you could have been here!" Cute, huh? But misguided. God is here. For thirty-three years Jesus, God's Son, lived here on the earth as a human person. His life and teachings are found in *Matthew, Mark, Luke,* and *John,* the first four books of the New Testament. Those books are called the Gospels, which means "good news."

Good news? Because Adam and Eve sinned against him, God sent his own Son to make things right again. Jesus did that by living a sinless life (something we couldn't do), dying on the cross for our sins, coming back to life, and returning to heaven to prepare a place for us. That's good news!

How much do you know about the life of Jesus, God's Son? Read all about it in the Gospels! And here's some more good news—when Jesus went back to heaven, he sent us the Holy Spirit. God is still here with us and always will be.

85

LEARNING THE BOOKS—
HISTORY AND LETTERS (EPISTLES)

Let's learn the next books of the New Testament.

- Acts (of the Apostles)
- Romans
- 1 Corinthians
- 2 Corinthians
- Galatians
- Ephesians
- Philippians
- Colossians
- 1 Thessalonians
- 2 Thessalonians
- 1 Timothy

- 2 Timothy
- Titus
- Philemon
- Hebrews
- James
- 1 Peter
- 2 Peter
- 1 John
- 2 John
- 3 John
- Jude

The book of Acts contains the history of the early church. (No, I don't mean the 8:00 a.m. worship service!) This book describes the experiences of the first believers and how they spread the good news about Jesus.

The other books—from Romans to Jude—are known as *epistles* (meaning "letters"). Many were letters written to churches within different cities (for instance, the church in Corinth) or to an individual (like the letters the apostle Paul wrote to Timothy). So if you're complaining because you never get any mail, take time to read a letter God has written to you today!

Let the word of Christ
dwell in you richly.
COLOSSIANS 3:16

Some people seem to be afraid of the words in the last book in the Bible—the book of Revelation—because it describes the judgments of God and talks about difficult things that will happen in the future. But they wouldn't be afraid if they knew that Revelation is really about the victory that Jesus has won over the devil and about the gift of heaven he has for all believers of every tribe, language, and race!

The book of Revelation is written in a style that is very different from the rest of the Bible. Some of it is difficult to understand because it contains a great deal of symbolism. Other parts seem very clear. The apostle John received and recorded this revelation about heaven.

Also in the book of Revelation Jesus says:

> Here I am! I stand at the door and knock.
> If anyone hears my voice and opens the door,
> I will come in and eat with him, and he with me.
>
> REVELATION 3:20

Don't be afraid! He wants to assure you that you will be safe if you are holding his hand.

ARE YOU COLOR-BLIND?

Dogs are color-blind.

Since finding this out, I stopped buying color-coordinated clothes for my dog, Duke. And no more green and orange dog food!

Spell *dog* backward and you'll discover someone else who is color-blind—God! His love isn't based on how someone looks, what colors a person wears, or the color of someone's skin.

Humans aren't fully color-blind. We not only notice color but often make choices based on color. This is not pleasing to God.

Paul wrote:

You are all children of God by believing in Christ Jesus. All of you who were baptized into Christ have put on Christ as if he were your clothes. There is no Jew or Greek. There is no slave or free person. There is no male or female. Because you belong to Christ Jesus, you are all one.

GALATIANS 3:26-28 NIrV

Wouldn't it be great if we saw everyone else just as we are—forgiven sinners, loved by God, dressed in Christ, and a reflection of his color-blind eyes of compassion?

RELATIVES IN
HIGH PLACES

Someone discovered that the artist Vincent van Gogh had many relatives. Among them were:

➡ his brother who worked at a convenience store—Stop N. Gogh
➡ his cousin from Illinois—Chica Gogh
➡ his grandfather who was a magician—Wherediddy Gogh
➡ his brother who loved prunes—Gotta Gogh
➡ his little bouncing nephew—Poe Gogh
➡ his niece who traveled the country in a van—Winnie Bay Gogh

Van Gogh wasn't the only one with famous relatives. Jesus and John the Baptist were related. God planned for John to be a special person to prepare the way for his relative, Jesus, who was coming to save the world. John's ministry was to point everyone to Jesus.

That is also our ministry. Did you know you have a ministry? You do. It's to point people to the Savior, Jesus, who loves them.

It's great to have relatives in high places! God is our Father. Jesus is our Brother. And we are part of the family that points others to him.

I'M SO EMBARRASSED

What was your most embarrassing moment?

Pharaoh must have been embarrassed when the Lord used Moses to get his people out of Egypt. The Lord sent lots of plagues but Pharaoh couldn't do anything about it. Pharaoh thought he was so great but then he met our God. It was God who sent plagues of blood in the Nile River (you may have red about it), frogs (eventually they all croaked), gnats (that would bug me), a plague on the live-stock (that was a baaaaad plague), boils (the people were in hot water with this one), hail (they weren't the size of golf balls—golf wasn't invented yet!), locusts (the first Buzzzzzz Lightyears), a plague of darkness (that was no light plague), and the plague on the firstborn. We have an awesome God! Don't be embarrassed to know him!

Remember what Paul wrote:

> I am not ashamed of the gospel, because it is the power of God for the salvation of everyone who believes.
>
> ROMANS 1:16

If you were King David, how would you have written Psalm 150? What would you have been bubbling over to praise God for? Read Psalm 150 in your Bible, then fill in the blanks with your own words of praise to the Lord.

Praise the LORD! Praise him in his _____!

Praise him in his _____!

Praise him for _____!

Praise him because he is _____!

Praise him by _____!

Praise him with _____ and _____!

Praise him with _____!

Praise him with _____!

Let everything that has _____ praise the LORD!

Praise the LORD!

PSALM 150

Didn't that feel good? Try using different words to fill in the blanks each day. Your "praise meter" will go through the roof!

Dear Dr. Devo,

Why is Song of Songs a book
in the Bible? It doesn't
seem to be about God. I'm
embarrassed not to know,
and sometimes I'm even
embarrassed to read it!

Signed,

Embarrassed

Dear Embarrassed,

*Don't be embarrassed! You
might be surprised to learn that
a lot of other people wonder the
same thing. Song of Songs (or Song
of Solomon, as it's known in some
Bibles) is a book of loving words and
poetry between a man and a woman.
It's a description of how deeply God
wants us to know and love him—
and how deeply he loves us.
Christian believers are sometimes
called "the bride of Christ."*

*We shouldn't be embar-
rassed to tell Jesus how
much we love him as he tells and shows us the same.*

In Christian love,
Dr. Devo

FEEL LIKE HAVING RIBS TONIGHT?

A young boy read in Genesis how God created Eve using one of Adam's ribs. Later that night he looked sick. His mom asked him, "Are you feeling okay?"

"No," he said. "I have a pain in my side. I think I'm going to have a wife."

You don't need to be thinking about marriage now, but the future is something for you and your parents to pray about. Add these thoughts to your prayer list:

- ➡ God, keep me faithful to your Word, will, and ways.
- ➡ God, give me wisdom for daily life and for my school years.
- ➡ God, use me to do your will in all the days ahead.
- ➡ God, work in the life of the person I might be married to one day.

Pray this way regularly. Read the following verse, then put your future into God's hands and enjoy this day that God has created for you! He will take care of the rest.

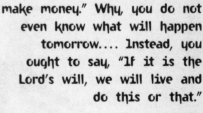

Now listen, you who say, "Today or tomorrow we will go to this or that city, spend a year there, carry on business and make money." Why, you do not even know what will happen tomorrow.... Instead, you ought to say, "If it is the Lord's will, we will live and do this or that."

JAMES 4:13-15

YOU'RE IN THE ARMY NOW

Question: Where does the king keep his armies?

Answer: In his sleevies!

On the way out of church after an Easter service, Pastor Tom shook Mr. Moore's hand. Then the pastor said, "Sir, you need to join the army of the Lord!"

Mr. Moore said, "I'm already in the army of the Lord, Pastor."

The pastor responded, "How come I only see you on Christmas and Easter?"

Mr. Moore whispered, "I'm in the secret service!"

That's funny, but in one sense it's not. I wonder if Mr. Moore would be ashamed if his friends knew he went to church where the army of the King of Kings met and worshiped.

Jesus said:

> If anyone is ashamed of me and my words ... the Son of Man will be ashamed of him when he comes in his Father's glory with the holy angels.
>
> **MARK 8:38**

Forgive us, King, when we act like we are ashamed to know you!

We want to be in your service, but not in secret!

Onward, Christian soldiers!

LAZYBONES

A teacher told her class, "I've got an easy job today for my laziest student. Will the laziest person please put up your hand?"

All but one hand went up. When asked why he didn't raise his hand, the student responded, "Too much trouble!"

Has anyone ever said you were lazy? If so, maybe you didn't think much about it. God warns us not to be lazy but rather he wants us to work hard when it comes to homework, doing chores, or having a job. The Bible also teaches us not to get lazy when it comes to our faith. We should look forward to Bible studies, devotions, and times of worship. We need to treasure our faith and not become lazy in growing closer to our God who loves us so much that his Son died so we can live.

Can you name some non-lazy, faithful people in the Bible?

> **We do not want you to become lazy, but to imitate those who through faith and patience inherit what has been promised.**
>
> HEBREWS 6:12

Ladies and gentlemen!

May I have your attention, please? It's time for the 487th greatest muscle show on earth. Instructions: Take time for each family member to put on a short demonstration, highlighting his or her best muscle forms. For more fun, think of goofy names for each performer. Afterward decide on the winner by applause and then finish the devotion.

Ladies and gentlemen! May God have your attention, please? He has some words to share.

First, in this corner, with a very muscular message, is Psalm 28:7:

> The LORD is my strength and my shield;
> my heart trusts in him, and I am helped.

And in this corner, check out these powerful words from Psalm 29:11:

> The LORD gives strength to his people; the LORD blesses his people with peace.

These verses show us that God likes to show off his muscles, too—to help us. If you don't have the strength to stop lying, cheating, being mean or negative—whatever—the Lord will give you his strength! That deserves a standing ovation!

A NEW SONG

The author of Psalm 149 wrote in verse 1:

Praise the LORD. Sing to the LORD a new song.

Even if you aren't a singer, you can at least make a joyful noise to the Lord! Take an easy song—one you've known since you were small—and rewrite the words to praise the Lord.

I'll show you how easy it is. I picked the tune "Row, Row, Row Your Boat" and wrote these words in just fifty-three seconds.

Sing, sing, sing a song;
Sing a song of praise.
To our God who reigns above;
A song of joy we'll raise!

Okay, it's not a masterpiece but it's a new song that gives God praise. Now it's your turn!

To get you thinking creatively, check out these old hymns that could be used as theme songs for different groups.

For dentists: "Crown Him with Many Crowns"
For architects and builders: "The Church's One Foundation"
For golfers: "There Is a Green Hill Far Away"
For clothes makers and tailors: "Holy, Holy, Holy"
For shoppers: "Sweet By and By"

YOU WANT TO ARGUE, DON'T YOU?

Do not! Do too! Do not! Do too!

A pastor saw an ad for miniature crosses made out of palm leaves. He ordered enough for each family in his congregation. The weekend they arrived, he told the congregation, "I have a little cross for each family. I want you to put it up in the room where your family argues the most. When you look at the cross, it will remind you that God is watching." As people were leaving the church, a woman shook that pastor's hand and said, "I'll take six, please."

Does that sound like your house sometimes—arguments in every room? The Bible says:

> Hate stirs up fights. But love erases
> all sins by forgiving them.
>
> **PROVERBS 10:12 NIrV**

I'm not suggesting that you hate your family members. But maybe you hate what God loves—patience and forgiveness. Without them fights are guaranteed.

Maybe before tomorrow's devotions you'll want to take some time making simple crosses to put in some of the rooms of your house.

QUIET TIME—
PANTOMIME TIME

It's pantomime time!

Act out (by yourself and without saying anything) the following Bible stories and see if your family can guess them.

1. Mary and Joseph traveling to Bethlehem to give birth to Jesus
2. The Lord's Supper in the Upper Room the night before Jesus died
3. The resurrection of Jesus

There is a time to talk and a time to be quiet. Yes, we want to tell unbelievers about the hope and help that Jesus brings. But there are times to be quiet so we don't sin—like when we are with people who don't believe in God. Being quiet might be a great witness to them. We could end up saying something hurtful instead of words that are helpful. Pray that you will know when to speak and when to be quiet.

> I will watch my ways and keep my tongue from sin;
> I will put a muzzle on my mouth as long as the
> wicked are in my presence.
>
> PSALM 39:1

People in Prison

Our prisons are filled with people who are hurting and who have hurt others. We need to pray for them. They desperately need our prayers and so do the victims of their crimes. Forgiveness, hope, and wisdom are needed for all those involved. Here's a starter list:

⟶ prison chaplains
⟶ warden and guards
⟶ families of those in prison
⟶ wisdom for parole boards
⟶ that those in prison would be sorry for their sin and come to know Jesus as their Savior
⟶ the victims of those who have been hurt by the prisoners
⟶ those imprisoned in other countries for sharing the good news of Jesus
⟶ wisdom for judges and juries
⟶ children and teens in prison
⟶ prison Bible studies

You may not even know anyone who is in prison, but if you do, pray for that person by name. Remember this Scripture:

Is any one of you in trouble?
He should pray.

JAMES 5:13

DR. DEVO'S
ADVICE COLUMN

Dear Dr. Devo,

I have some questions for you.

How could Methuselah live to be 969 years old?

Why didn't Enoch die? It says, "He was no more, because God took him away" (Genesis 5:24).

Was Noah's son, named Ham, the first actor because he was always a ham?

Why did God choose the size of the ark to be 450 feet long, 75 feet wide, and 45 feet high?

Signed,

Just Wondering

Dear Just Wondering,

Here are the answers to your questions.

I don't know. I really couldn't say. I'm not sure. I have no idea.

Signed,

Dr. Devo

P.S. There are some things that we just don't know or understand. They don't matter as long as we understand God's love for us. I guess you'll have to ask God when you get to heaven. But when you're there, those questions probably won't matter anyway.

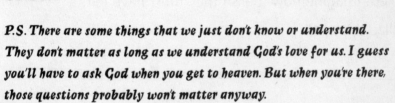

TRICK OR TREAT

Question 1: Fill in the blank—Frank's father has three sons: Snap, Crackle, and _____?

Answer: Frank!

Question 2: A cowboy rode to an inn (motel) on Friday. He stayed two nights and left on Friday. How could that be? (Give some time for guesses.)

Answer: His horse was named Friday!

Those are tricky questions but they're just for fun! When it comes to serious questions, I bet you don't like being tricked. None of us do.

The Pharisees were always following Jesus around, trying to trick him into sin. Of course, they couldn't do it. He was perfect—sinless. But they kept trying. I think they must have gone home feeling like they were the ones who had been tricked. Imagine how foolish they must have felt.

Realize this truth:

Don't be fooled. You can't outsmart God.

GALATIANS 6:7 NIrV

102

COUNTRYSIDE PRAYERS

Fill in the blanks with countries to complete the sentences. (Answers are below.)

1. The temperature outside is dropping, so you might get _____ today.
2. On our cruise to Alaska, we saw some incredible _____ swimming near the boat.
3. You just stood there when _____.
4. I use one _____ sugar to _____ my coffee.
5. Honey, did you break my good _____ plate?
6. Not only did Jon gyp you, but _____ me too!

God wants to use us to take his good news to these nations and all the world. The Bible says:

> Rejoice greatly, O Daughter of Zion! Shout, Daughter of Jerusalem! See, your king comes to you, righteous and having salvation.... He will proclaim peace to the nations. His rule will extend from sea to sea and from the River to the ends of the earth.
>
> ZECHARIAH 9:9-10

Let today's prayers include the people in the countries above. Include pastors, missionaries, those being persecuted because of their Christian faith, families, and the leaders of the countries.

Answers: 1-Chile; 2-Wales; 3-Iran; 4-Cuba, Sweden; 5-China; 6-Egypt.

ON THE GROW

It's riddle time!

A king wants an honest child to take his place on the throne. He gives each of his three sons a pack of flower seeds and tells them that the one who grows the most beautiful flowers from these seeds will have his throne. Six months later the king checks his sons' flowers. The first two had beautiful flower beds, while his last son had no flowers in his plot. Yet the king chose this child to have the throne. Why?

Answer: The king baked the flower seeds before giving them to his sons so they wouldn't grow. This means the first two sons didn't use the seeds their father gave them. The third son was the only one that didn't cheat.

Like the king in the riddle, the King of Kings, Jesus, wants honest followers, upstanding children.

> I haven't told any lies. My feet haven't hurried to cheat others. So let God weigh me in honest scales. Then he'll know I haven't done anything wrong.
>
> JOB 31:5-6 NIrV

WHAT'S YOUR CAP SIZE?

Question 1: Which football player wears the biggest helmet?

- **a.** the quarterback
- **b.** the linebacker
- **c.** the fullback
- **d.** the one with the biggest head

Question 2: "You have a big head!" is also a description (that isn't very nice) of people who are:

- **a.** egotistical
- **b.** cocky
- **c.** self-centered
- **d.** thinking too highly of themselves
- **e.** all of the above

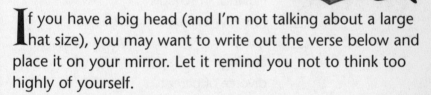

The answers are 1-*d*, 2-*e*.

If you have a big head (and I'm not talking about a large hat size), you may want to write out the verse below and place it on your mirror. Let it remind you not to think too highly of yourself.

> God's grace has been given to me. So here is what I say to every one of you. Don't think of yourself more highly than you should. Be reasonable when you think about yourself.
>
> ROMANS 12:3 NIrV

Remember that Jesus had a crown of thorns on his head for those who think about themselves too much . . . and not enough about him.

WHAT'S WORSE?

Here is a quiz to give your parents. It's called "What's Worse?" What do they think is the worst situation of the five? Which do you think they'll pick?

1. finding a moldy cup under your preteen's bed
2. your preteen having a new saying . . . and saying it constantly!
3. the telephone ringing every five minutes for your child
4. trying to relate to the music your child listens to but not being able to understand the words
5. realizing that a best friend of your child has a one word vocabulary—and it's "Huh?"

Try this with your family. How would each one of you rate the most difficult things preteens (ages 8–12) deal with in your community (with 1 being the most difficult or important issue)?

___ violence in schools
___ music with a bad message
___ gangs
___ cussing
___ divorce of parents
___ sex issues
___ peer pressure
___ lack of respect for others
___ need to look and be the best
___ anger

Talk and pray together about these issues!

Mrs. Teachum noticed that one of her students was upset. At recess Mrs. Teachum called her over so they could talk. "Ima! Ima Fibbin! Come here, please!" Ima slowly walked over to her teacher. "What's the matter, Ima?" asked the teacher.

Ima hung her head and mumbled, "Mrs. Teachum, everyone thinks I'm a liar."

The teacher put her arm around Ima Fibbin and said, "Well I can't believe that!"

It might be easy for you to think of someone else who seems to lie a lot (and I don't mean lie on a bed)! But let's each look at our own lives and lies. Then look at the life and strife of Jesus, who died so liars can be changed through his forgiveness and power. Then pray what Solomon prayed. One of Solomon's wise prayers was very simple:

Keep lies far away from me.
PROVERBS 30:8 NIrV

THE BLAME GAME

People like to play the blame game. It sounds like this:

"She did it!"

"He made me do it!"

"Did not! She made me!"

"Did not!" (And so forth)

When Adam and Eve sinned, they blamed each other. Their blame game is in Genesis 3:8–13.

We all sin! We need to stop blaming others and admit what we have done. Thankfully, God sent Jesus to clean up our mess. Paul wrote:

> Christ didn't have any sin. But God made him become sin for us. So we can be made right with God because of what Christ has done for us.
>
> 2 CORINTHIANS 5:21 NIrV

Dear God, Please take care of our family and friends. Thanks for saving us from the big mess our sin got us into, Jesus. You took the blame for us! I love your love. Amen.

GOING OUT

Question 1: What did the big candle say to the little candle?

Answer: You're too young to go out!

Question 2: What would your parents say if you wanted to go to an R-rated movie or spend a few hours at a carnival with a friend?

Answer: Maybe they'd say, "Remember what the big candle said to the little candle!"

You won't always agree with your parents' answers. But God wants parents to raise children in his ways, to love them, and to guide them in making good choices. He asks children to obey and respect their parents in return. Paul wrote:

> Children, obey your parents as believers in the Lord.
> Obey them because it's the right thing to do.
>
> EPHESIANS 6:1 NIrV

Be thankful your parents have rules, even when they say, "You're too young to go out." They only want what is best, because they love you! So does your heavenly Father!

MEOW! CALLING ALL FRAIDY CATS!

Let's all complete this sentence:

I'm a fraidy cat when it comes to _____.

What are the top five things or people or situations that you are afraid of?

1. _____
2. _____
3. _____
4. _____
5. _____

A phobia is a great fear of something.
Match the fear with the phobia name.
(Answers are below.)

1. acrophobia _____ **a.** fear of dust
2. ailurophobia _____ **b.** fear of meat
3. amathophobia _____ **c.** fear of cats
4. blennophobia _____ **d.** fear of slime
5. carnophobia _____ **e.** fear of heights

Look up these fearless verses and fill in the blanks. Pray the message of the verses for your lives.

Genesis 26:24: "Do not be _____, for ___ am _____ you."
Deuteronomy 1:21: "Do not be _____; do not be
_____." Psalm 56:3: "When I am _____, I will
_____ ____ _____." Psalm 34:4: "I sought the LORD,
and he answered me; he delivered me from _____ my _____."

Phobia answers: 1-*e*, 2-*c*, 3-*a*, 4-*d*, 5-*b*.

Those Who Are Sick

It's no fun being sick. You probably know many people who are sick today whom you could pray for by name—and I hope you do—from people with headaches to colds to heart problems to cancer.

Have you ever thought about how they treated people in Bible times when they didn't have the medicine God has gifted us with today?

→ Skin diseases: mineral baths or ointments and pastes made of herbs and oils
→ Boils: a hot fig paste
→ Wounds: salt to clean and disinfect; olive oil and wine
→ Stomachs and internal problems: medicines made from roots, pounded into powder, and boiled leaves and berries

Yuck! Medicine may not always taste good but God uses it to heal us. He also answers prayers.

> Are any of you sick? Then send for the elders of the church to pray over you.
>
> JAMES 5:14 NIrV

Prayer is the most powerful medicine of all!

DR. DEVO'S ADVICE COLUMN

Dear Dr. Devo,

I'm scared of girls. That's it. Girls. Now I've said it. I'm scared of girls.

Signed,

Scared of girls

Dear Scared,

I'm trying to think of what advice to give you. When I read your letter, I thought of this poem:

> I pressed a kiss to her lips,
> What could I do but linger.
> And as I ran my hand through her hair—
> A cootie bit my finger!

You don't have to be scared because cooties aren't real.

The Bible doesn't say anything specific about boys being scared of girls. But there are many times when God says, "Do not be afraid." I don't think there is anything to be scared of with girls in general. So I would say, read some of the "do not be afraid" stories in the Bible (like Luke 1:11–13; 26–30; Mark 5:24–34) and then pray about your frightful female fear.

Be calm,

Dr. Devo

CONTACT THE COMPLAINT DEPARTMENT

This word game is called spoonerisms. By switching words or a letter in each sentence, a totally different meaning appears. (Answers are below.)

Example: A dentist yanks for the roots. A New York baseball fan roots for the Yanks.

1. A fast cyclist is a speeding _____. A book-loving web-spinner is a _____ _____.

2. Sacks of coins are money _____. Rabbit periodicals are _____ _____.

3. Rabbit fur is bunny _____. A sweet-toothed grizzly is a _____ _____.

4. An adorable glove is a cute _____. A silent baby cat is a _____ _____.

Two words that are easy to get mixed up are *compliment* and *complaint*. They look similar on the page. Our problem is that we complain a lot more than we give compliments. One way not to get the words (or their meanings) mixed up is to stop complaining and start complimenting!

Encourage one another daily.
HEBREWS 3:13

Answers: 1—speeding rider, reading spider; 2—money bags, bunny mags; 3—bunny hair, honey bear; 4—cute mitten, mute kitten

MICROWAVE YOUR WORDS

Word game time! Match the description on the right with the appropriate word on the right.

1. microwave
2. goblet
3. dandelion
4. hatchet
5. appeal

_____ **a.** what a hen does with an egg
_____ **b.** a wonderful king of the jungle
_____ **c.** a little farewell
_____ **d.** outside layer of a banana
_____ **e.** a little turkey

That's a fun way to use words. There are other words that people think are funny but they aren't. Those words are used to cuss, call people names, and tell dirty jokes. Think about this:

> There must not be any unclean speech or foolish talk or dirty jokes. All of them are out of place. Instead, you should give thanks.
>
> EPHESIANS 5:4 NIrV

God doesn't want us to use hurtful words or cuss words. Our words should give God thanks!

Answers: 1-d, 2-c, 3-a, 4-e, 5-b.

ORDER, PLEASE

What is the holiday message found in the order of the letters below?

**A B C D E F G H 1 J K
M N O P Q R S T U V W X Y Z**

You've probably heard people talk about the day when Jesus will return. You might have questions about what will happen on that day. Read 1 Thessalonians 4:13–18 NIrV and check the order. Can you memorize these in order?

"The Lord himself will come down from heaven."

"We will hear a loud command."

"We will hear the voice of the leader of the angels."

"We will hear a blast from God's trumpet."

"Many who believe in Christ will have died already. They will rise first."

"We who are still alive and are left will be caught up together with them."

"We will be taken up in the clouds."

"We will meet the Lord in the air."

"We will be with him forever."

That is great news!

Answer: Noel! (No L.)

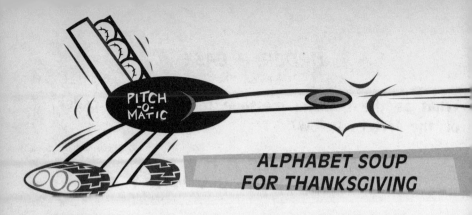

ALPHABET SOUP FOR THANKSGIVING

Today is a great day to be happy and give God thanks! [Aren't all days?]

> This is the day the LORD has made;
> let us rejoice and be glad in it.
>
> PSALM 118:24

Hand out a piece of paper and a pen or pencil to each family member. Use each letter of the alphabet to make a list of things or people or events for which you are thankful. This is called an anagram. For instance, *A* stands for Aunt Ruth, for whom you are thankful. *B* reminds me to be thankful for my brain! Now it's your turn!

After everyone creates their own thanksgiving list, compare the lists.

If you're ever in a bad mood or think that nothing is going your way, this is a simple way to get your mind back to realizing how you are blessed. This is a day of rejoicing and thanksgiving!

Thank you, Lord, for all your blessings, especially the gift of our Savior and his gifts. Amen.

SHOULD I PASS IT ON?

You may have played the game called telephone. It starts with the person reading this devotion. The reader whispers the sentence below to another person, and they whisper it to another, until it gets back to the first person. Usually the message changes a lot before it returns to the original sender! Give it a try.

Whisper this to the person next to you:

"There was once a moose who ran away to be with his mother's brother, whose name was Mud."

So how did it work? Did the sentence come back exactly the same? Usually our words don't. That's one of the reasons it's wrong to gossip or pass on a rumor about someone else. A rumor is a story about someone that you don't really know is true. In passing it on to others, you could be passing on a lie about someone. It could hurt their reputation, feelings, and friendships. If we are going to talk about other people, let's pass on true, encouraging, and kind things.

A gossip separates close friends.

PROVERBS 16:28

Daffynitions are silly, punny definitions of regular words. Have fun with these.

- → buccaneer—how much cheap earrings cost
- → alarms—what an octopus looks like
- → vitamin—what you do when a friend knocks on your door
- → khaki—the metal object you use to start a car
- → pasteurize—too far for you to see

These daffynitions are funny. But some words aren't funny, and it's especially important to understand their real meaning. In a movie or TV program, have you ever seen men and women living together like they are married, but they aren't? In the Bible this is referred to as immorality. The Bible says:

Flee from sexual immorality.... You were bought at a price. Therefore honor God with your body.

1 CORINTHIANS 6:18, 20

God's Word and what is on TV or in movies often don't agree. But God knows what is best and he says immorality is a sin.

From the Dr. Devo riddle department:

Marco was watching TV late one night while his sister, Sally, was reading a book. They were sitting together on a sofa. Suddenly the electricity went out and Marco went to bed because the TV didn't work. His sister kept reading. There was no artificial, candle, or emergency lighting, and it was very dark outside. How was Sally able to keep reading?

Answer: Sally's blind. She was reading a book in Braille.

Braille is a way for blind people to read. The letters are made by different bumps on paper. By moving your fingers over the bumps, you can read!

That's a handy way to use your hands. Are your hands handy in a good or bad way? Ever want to hit your brother or sister? Ever want to use your hands to throw something at someone? Remember:

Do not repay anyone evil for evil.
ROMANS 12:17

How can God use your hands to help others? How did Jesus use his hands to change your life?

WHAT'S ON YOUR PLATE?

It's fun to read special license plates on cars. They describe the driver, their car, or their work. They are called "vanity plates," and shout "Look at me!" Vanity has to do with thinking too much of yourself, being proud of yourself, rather than giving God the praise.

Match these vanity license plates with the owners they describe. (Answers are below.)

1.	4CAST	_____	**a.**	surgeon
2.	IC2020	_____	**b.**	dentist
3.	IOPER8	_____	**c.**	tennis player
4.	MOOTEL	_____	**d.**	eye doctor
5.	2THDR	_____	**e.**	weather person
6.	10SNE1	_____	**f.**	dairy farmer

There's nothing wrong with having vanity plates, unless they are boastful in a sinful way. God wants us to be humble. He also wants us to share his message. Maybe we should use those plates to share Jesus with others. Here are some ideas.

4GIVEN   PSALM46   ESD14U!

Answers: 1-*e*, 2-*d*, 3-*a*, 4-*f*, 5-*b*, 6-*c*.

When pride comes, then comes disgrace,
but with humility comes wisdom.

PROVERBS 11:2

DR. DEVO'S ADVICE COLUMN

Dear Dr. Devo,

My best friend, Grace, moved to another town last month with her family. I miss her so much. Grace and I had so much fun together. She knew all my secrets. She was like a sister to me. Help!

Signed,

Missing Grace

Dear Missing Grace,

A good friend who loves at all times is a wonderful gift from God (Proverbs 17:17). Keep in touch with her as best you can.

Since you'll have more time now that Grace has moved, maybe you can spend it making sure the people around you don't miss the grace of God. That's what Hebrews 12:15 says to do. Grace means "undeserved love." You were blessed with the undeserved gift of a friend named Grace, plus the best gift from your best friend, Jesus—his grace that has saved you. Have fun living in God's grace!

Gracefully signed,

Dr. Devo

Caregivers

Patient 1: "Doctor, Doctor, I feel like a pair of curtains!"

Doctor: "Relax! Just pull yourself together."

Patient 2: "Doctor, Doctor, I feel like a deck of cards!"

Doctor: "I'll deal with you later."

Those keep me in stitches! Time now for doctor trivia: Which New Testament author was a doctor? (Colossians 4:14 has the answer.)

There are so many different people who care for those who are sick. Although they do it because they love to help others, it can be an exhausting job—for their bodies and their minds. Here are some prayer suggestions as you lift caregivers up to the Lord in prayer.

→ doctors
→ nurses
→ nursing home workers
→ those caring for sick or elderly family members
→ hospice care workers
→ hospital chaplains
→ those in ministry with the mentally handicapped
→ military medical teams
→ missionary medical workers

If you can, let caregivers know you are praying for them. As Paul wrote:

You help us by your prayers.
2 CORINTHIANS 1:11

PUTTING YOU ON THE SPOT

Take turns answering these questions:

1. If you could have a place in your house—just for you—what would it look like?
2. Why would you want a private spot? What would you do there?
3. Do you think there is anything wrong with wanting to be alone?

God wants us to have relationships—parents and children, brothers and sisters, friends, neighbors, classmates. But most people also like some time alone. Maybe you have a special spot that only you and God know about. He loves being with you wherever you are.

Jesus often needed a quiet spot—a place where he could be alone to rest and to pray to his Father. One time was after he had a very tiring day with crowds of people. Jesus told the disciples to go on without him for a while, and then he spent some time in prayer.

> **He went up on a mountainside by himself to pray.**
> MATTHEW 14:23

Enjoy whatever quiet time and special spot you have. You'll probably enjoy it even more if you spend some time talking with your heavenly Father.

A LAW RAP

God's law shows us our sins, which reminds us we need a Savior. The Bible says,

Blessed is he who keeps the law.
PROVERBS 29:18

Here's a law rap—rap it with style!

My name is Law and this is my story.
Don't follow me? You'll have to say, "Sorry!"
But follow the rules and all will be cool.
The laws of our God for home and at school.
I'll show you your sins—that's what I'm about.
And bring on guilt that'll make you pout.
You need me for the straight and narrow,
For Satan wants you, right down to your marrow.
So don't play games with faith in your Lord.
Respect me, Law, and don't get bored.
God gives his commands out of love for you.
Remember that as you follow him, true.
If you only live with laws to follow,
*   In helplessness surely you will wallow.*
*   Don't forget what follows God's great Law:*
*   The gospel—good news—you'll drop*
*   your jaw!*

A GOSPEL (GOOD NEWS) RAP

The Bible says:

> By this gospel you are saved.
>
> 1 CORINTHIANS 15:2

Rap this, dude or dudette!

My name is Gospel and this is my story.
It's a great grace story that ends hunky-dory.
I'll show you your Savior—his name is Jesus.
You want to know him and everything he does.
Forgiveness he brings, also life and salvation.
His love for you never takes a vacation.
But when you fall into sin and shame is your game,
Run to Jesus, your Savior, and call on his name.
He took your sins and shame to the cross.
Into "Forgetful Land" he gave them a toss.
The Father, Son, and Holy Spirit
Love you, so be glad to hear it!
Spread the news that the Gospel's in the land
As Jesus lifts you up with his nail-scarred hand.
So this is Gospel's story—never doubt God's love.
Your salvation is why he came from above.
Now this is the last line of our rap,
But beware, kids—it doesn't even rhyme!

ON A MISSION—
FEASTING ON GOD'S WORD

Have you noticed that some restaurants have newspapers for people to read—especially while they have breakfast? But have you ever seen a person or family read devotions at a restaurant?

I wonder if those restaurants would allow you to do some mission work there. You could buy an extra copy of *Dr. Devo's Lickety-Split Devotions* (or any other devotional book or magazine) and ask the restaurant if you could place it with their newspapers. What a great mission field! Many of the people who eat there may not know about God's love, forgiveness, and gift of heaven through Jesus, or they may have forgotten the importance of that relationship.

God may want to use you for this unique mission field in your community. People need the Lord—it's a matter of life and death. Maybe you and your family have other creative ways to tell your world about Jesus, who is the only way to heaven.

Talk about it and pray that the Lord would give you ideas about how to share his story.

All hands on board for a cabinet food search! Check for labels that say things like, "reduces the risk of heart disease" or "reduces cholesterol" or "high in fiber." Bring the items to the table and read the statements out loud. (Go ahead! I'll wait.)

Do you believe the statement?

Does the statement make you want to eat more of the product?

Jesus told Martha (whose brother died):

> 1 am the resurrection and the life. He who believes in me will live, even though he dies; and whoever lives and believes in me will never die. Do you believe this?
>
> JOHN 11:25-26

How would you answer if Jesus made that statement to you? How would you respond?

Would you feel comfortable saying to others, "Faith in Jesus Christ will not only reduce the risk of death but eliminate it"? That's very sweet news!

Words to put to memory:

> Taste and see that the LORD is good.
>
> PSALM 34:8

BORING

Do you feel like your life is one big bowl of Boring Cereal? I know a girl who did—until one day!

Mary had a boring life;
She hated her behavior.
She sulked through days of yucky stuff;
But then she met her Savior!
He followed her to school one day;
She wondered what to think.
But Jesus said he'd always stay—
To make her life not stink!

If you think you have a boring life, Jesus wants to spice it up. Jesus came to bring you a life that is overflowing with a special joy! He told his disciples:

> **I have come that they may have life,**
> **and have it to the full.**
> **JOHN 10:10**

Jesus will be with you today, wherever you go. He promises that he will never leave you or forget about you. He wants to bring you a day full of his kind of joyful life!

Hey! Fill up your bowl with another helping of anything but Boring while Jesus is filling your day with joy.

SOGGY FLAKES ARE GREAT

Imagine a TV commercial for a cereal called Soggy Flakes. Ready? Action!

(A brother and sister are seated at a table with a bowl of cereal on it. They take turns eating.)

Sis: This cereal is soggy.

Bro: I like it that way.

Sis: It tastes gross.

Bro: It's just right. Who wants crunchy flakes? Soggy is cool!

Sis: I want strong, crispy cereal. Let's get Mom to try it!

Mom (takes a bite): Mmmmmm. Soggy is cool!

Announcer: You heard it! Soggy is cool! Buy Soggy Flakes today!

Director: Cut! That's a wrap!

Yuck! That's just weird! Paul said something in the Bible that sounds a little weird, too:

> When I am weak, then I am strong.
>
> 2 CORINTHIANS 12:10

He didn't mind being weak (soggy), because that made him realize how much he needed God's strength.

Maybe you're not as fast or as tall or as strong as the other kids. When you're feeling a little weak and soggy, rely on God for strength. He's bigger and stronger than any problem.

Laughter is a great gift from God. In fact, let's laugh right now! Take turns trying to get the person sitting next to you to laugh. But here's the trick: You can't touch them. Try whatever you'd like but no touching! It's time for a laugh-in party!

Abraham and Sarah once had a laugh-in party. Sarah laughed at God when he told them they would have a baby. It must have sounded a little funny, because Abraham was a hundred and Sarah was ninety years old! They forgot that God can do anything. He always keeps his promises!

It's great to laugh but not at God! The people who crucified Jesus laughed at him. They laughed at who he said he was. How did he respond? He said:

> Father, forgive them, for they do not know what they are doing.
> LUKE 23:34

So laugh, laugh, and laugh some more—but not at God or his ways. Let him know that you will always trust him to keep his promises.

FALLING FADS
FADE FAST

A fad or trend is something that is really popular for a while and then people seem to forget about it. Here are some fads that have popped up over the years. Have a family vote on what you think the best fad of all time has been.

→ Pokéman cards
→ scooters
→ Cabbage Patch Dolls
→ Hula Hoops
→ Beanie Babies
→ Pet Rocks
→ Harry Potter collectibles

Every company wants to be a part of the hottest fads because they can make a lot of money in a short time. Kids want to be like their friends. Some adults want to collect trendy things in case they are worth more money someday.

There is one trend that will always be popular—it's God's Word and all the wonderful promises God has placed in it for you.

The grass withers
and the flowers fall,
but the word of the
Lord stands forever.

1 PETER 1:24-25

GIVING AND GETTING DIRECTIONS

If you had to give someone directions from your school to your house, could you do it? Do you know all the names of the streets you would have to take on the way? Do you know where to turn left or right? East or west? North or south?

Let's play a little game. Have a family member pick a spot, and see if he or she can get from where you are to that spot by following your directions. Now pick another spot and let another family member give the directions. Continue until every family member has had an opportunity to give and to follow the directions.

How did you do?

God has given us directions about how to get to heaven. As a family, work together, pretending you're giving someone directions to heaven. What would you tell them? One simple answer is to read John 14:6. Check that out after your family puts your directions together.

See you on the road— to heaven!

A PLANE OL' DEVOTION

Today is the annual Dr. Devo paper airplane long-distance flying contest, and it's being held at your house! Everyone gets one piece of paper to make a paper airplane. The winner is chosen by the distance the airplane flies. Only paper can be used.

Make your planes. Send them flying and then return to this devotion—lickety-split!

Since there weren't any rules about how the plane looked, someone could have just wadded up a piece of paper into a ball and thrown it as hard as possible. That probably would have won! Most people try to make a plane that looks good. Sometimes those that look the best don't fly the best.

Jesus warned the Pharisees about their looks. He told them they looked very "religious" on the outside but their insides were filled with evil. God knows what we're like inside and out.

Read and talk about Matthew 23:27–28 and thank God for the winning faith he has created inside you!

ANOTHER PLANE OL' DEVOTION

Today is another Dr. Devo paper airplane design contest, and it's being held at your house! Everyone gets one piece of paper to make an airplane. The winner will be the one who receives the most votes from his or her family members. This contest is based on how the plane looks, not on how well it flies. Make your planes, vote, and then return to this devotion—lickety-split!

In an airplane contest, looks matter. But in real life God doesn't judge people by the way they look. Plain-looking people, beautiful people, and even those who make beautiful-looking planes are all equal in God's sight.

When the Lord was looking for a king to lead his people, he told Samuel to ignore appearance, saying:

> The LORD does not look at the things man looks at. Man looks at the outward appearance, but the LORD looks at the heart.
>
> 1 SAMUEL 16:7

Just like the Lord, look for and enjoy the beauty in people's hearts.

NO SWEAT?

1. An average man on an average day sweats _____!

- **a.** three tablespoons
- **b.** three-quarters of a pint
- **c.** two and a half quarts
- **d.** buckets and buckets full

2. What parts of the body contain more sweat glands than any other?

- **a.** nose and ears
- **b.** palms of the hands and soles of the feet
- **c.** underarms and neck
- **d.** backs of knees and wrists

Answers: 1-c, 2-b

I have one more lickety-split, sweaty fact for you. When Jesus was heading to the cross for you and me, he stopped to pray in the Garden of Gethsemane. His prayer was so powerful, he was so into his prayer, he was facing so much agony, that the Bible tells us:

His sweat was like drops of blood falling to the ground.
LUKE 22:44

Jesus went through so much for us. What love! What a Savior! What sweet, sweaty news!

PRAYER PONDER POINT

Parents

Okay, kids, time to pray for your parents! They have the greatest job in the world— taking care of you. Their job is easy, right? No problem!

This could be the first time you've asked your parents the following questions. I wish I could see their faces.

"Mom, Dad, I'm going to pray for you. What are some things you would like me to pray about that you're dealing with right now? I'm sure it's no problem having me as a kid, but what can I (we) pray about to help you in your calling to be a parent?"

Now that you've asked, write down their answers, and then pray!

If one parents is not at home, maybe you could make a lickety-split phone call. If you have stepparents, ask them as well. If your mom or dad has died, say some special prayers for the one who is with you.

Remember the commandment:

> **Honor your father and your mother.**
> Exodus 20:12

One way to honor them is to lift them up in prayer.
Happy praying!

DR. DEVO'S ADVICE COLUMN

Dear Dr. Devo,

My brother is a pain in the neck. He gets everything he wants. That's not fair! I don't think my parents would even notice if I was gone. All they care about is my brother.

Signed,

Pained in the Neck

Dear Pained in the Neck,

The first thing I would suggest is to see a good chiropractor about that neck problem you have.

After that you should sit down with your parents and tell them how you feel. I'm sure they would notice if you were gone. Their first clue would be less laundry! Just joking! Let your parents know how you feel, and I think they'll let you know that they love and care for you very much! God has created everyone to be a special and unique person. Pray that you are able to show love to your brother and that he can share his caring heart with you.

In Christ's love,

Dr. Devo

P.S. Don't send me the chiropractor's bill but do read Proverbs 17:6.

I WANT IT!

If you could wave a wand and get one thing that your friend has, what would it be?

→ toy
→ video game
→ computer
→ bike
→ game
→ outfit
→ pet

The Israelites envied their neighbors and said:

We want a king over us. Then we will be like all the other nations, with a king to lead us and to go out before us and fight our battles.

1 SAMUEL 8:19-20

God was their king but they wanted an earthly king. God warned them that bad things would happen if they trusted in earthly people rather than trusting in him. But they insisted, so God said okay! And guess what? It was a very bad idea that caused a lot of trouble for a very long time.

It's never a good idea to keep asking for something that God says won't be good for you. Thank God for what he has given you!

Look around the room you're in. From what you see, what do you think would be the most difficult thing to put together? Pretend a new one was delivered to your house tomorrow unassembled—parts everywhere. What would be the most difficult to make?

(I'm waiting for answers!)

I wonder if any of you picked the human body! Guess how many living cells are in our bodies? If you guessed a jillion-zillion, you were close! There are ten trillion! And don't forget the seventy thousand miles of blood vessels! Wouldn't you have fun putting together the 206 different bones in someone's body?

David stood in awe of God's creation of the body and wrote:

> 1 praise you because 1 am fearfully and wonderfully made; your works are wonderful, 1 know that full well.
>
> PSALM 139:14

Let us praise God for the wonder of our bodies and all his marvelous works!

A NOTE ABOUT MUSIC

Music is a wonderful gift from God. But we also know there is a lot of music in our world that is not pleasing to God. In fact, there is some very bad music that is hurting the minds and lives of kids and adults. The words to some songs show disrespect to people, abuse God's name, encourage violence, express hatred, and sometimes even talk about killing yourself and others.

It's time to start remembering music, musicians, and listeners regularly in your prayers. Below are some prayer ideas to get you started. Please add others! Then pray for these people on your own or as a family.

As you consider the list, read any or all of these psalms of praise: Psalm 146, 147, 148, 149, 150.

➡ musicians in general
➡ church choir members and directors
➡ band members
➡ music store owners
➡ agents and producers for bands
➡ people writing lyrics (words)
➡ record companies
➡ church musicians
➡ that people who buy music will make wise, godly choices

WOMB FOR A MIRACLE

Question: What could you call twins before they are born?

Answer: Womb-mates (roommates)!

If you didn't get that joke, it might be because you don't know what a womb is. It's the part of a woman's body where her unborn baby lives.

Jesus' life on earth began in the womb of Mary. When an angel told Mary she would become pregnant, she was a little confused. How could it be? The angel told her not to be afraid. He said that the Holy Spirit would create the child within her.

Now imagine this: Mary is only a teenager, but she becomes suddenly calm, totally trusting God as she says:

> 1 am the Lord's servant....
> May it be to me as you have said.
> **LUKE 1:38**

Wow! That's amazing faith! She had room for a miracle, one as big as giving birth to the Savior of the world. Make room for God's miracles in your life!

Everyone probably knows these riddles.

Question 1: Why did the chicken cross the road?

Answer: To get to the other side.

Question 2: Why did the piece of gum cross the road?

Answer: It was stuck to the chicken's foot.

And everyone should know this one—if they don't, we need to tell them:

Question 3: Why did Jesus cross the road from the palace of Pontius Pilate to a hill called Golgotha or Calvary?

Answer: To get believers to the other side of this life and into heaven!

That one was no joke! Cross the road with Jesus! Stick with his ways! And don't be too chicken to tell others of the good news about him!

> Pilate handed him over to them to be crucified. So the soldiers took charge of Jesus. Carrying his own cross, he went out to the place of the Skull [which in Aramaic is called Golgotha].
>
> JOHN 19:16-17

THE OTHER SIDE OF THE COIN

Take a look at the little grooves around the edges of a quarter and a dime. It might seem obvious that since the quarter is larger than the dime, it would have more grooves—and it does! But only one more. There are 119 grooves on a quarter and 118 on a dime. Sometimes things aren't what they seem.

Now take a look at Jesus and his disciples just before he died, rose, and ascended into heaven. The disciples would obviously be very, very sad. But Jesus wanted them to know that he would bring good from this situation. His death would save people from their sins and give them the joy of heaven. Sometimes things aren't what they seem.

Jesus told his disciples:

Now is your time of grief, but I will see you again and you will rejoice, and no one will take away your joy.
JOHN 16:22

If you are sad about something now, God will show you the other side of the coin—the good that he will bring from it.

FACE-OFF

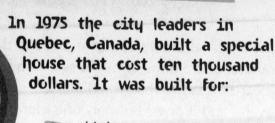

In 1975 the city leaders in Quebec, Canada, built a special house that cost ten thousand dollars. It was built for:

a. birds.

b. a dog.

c. a homeless family of seven.

d. the city leaders.

If you answered c, that would be a good guess but a wrong answer! Gotcha! The correct answer is a—birds!

All that money for a birdhouse! That's for the birds! Can you imagine anyone caring that much about birds? I can. And I don't mean the Quebec city leaders.

I'm thinking about our heavenly Father. Jesus reminded people that birds don't work or store up food in barns but God feeds them, takes care of them, and knows all about them. They are valuable to God because they are part of his creation. But Jesus then told the people:

> Are you not much more valuable than [birds]?
> MATTHEW 6:26

God the Father values you more than you can imagine. You are so loved that Jesus gave his life for you!

WHERE HAVE I SEEN AND HEARD THAT BEFORE?

Question 1: Where have you seen these letters—in this order?

QWERTYUIOP

Question 2: Did Jesus tell his disciples he would suffer, die, and rise from the dead?

The answer to the second question is yes. In fact, Jesus told them on three separate occasions. You would think that after hearing it three times, they wouldn't have been so upset when he died. They must have forgotten that he also told them three times that he would rise from the dead.

Getting back to the first question, the answer is the top row of letters on a computer keyboard. Many of you have seen that over and over and over again, but you may have forgotten.

> Again he took the Twelve aside and told them what was going to happen to him.
>
> MARK 10:32

Jesus, when I read and hear your words and promises, make them stick in my mind and heart so I'll never forget the love and hope you have given me. Amen.

Open your Bible to the Old Testament and find the name Lord. What's different about how it's printed? Most Bibles, not all, capitalize the letters: LORD.

Here's why: The Old Testament was written in Hebrew. In the Bible you will find many names for God. One of those names is LORD, which in Hebrew is Yahweh (pronounced "*Yah*-way"). What's so neat about this is that Yahweh was like God's personal name.

God was making a covenant, a pact, with his people. He would be their personal God and they would be his people. He wanted them to have a close, personal relationship with him. He told them to call him by his personal name, Yahweh, or LORD, or as he says in Exodus 3:14:

"I AM WHO I AM."

When *you* read his name—LORD— smile and remember, *That's my personal Lord and Savior! We're tight. We're so close, he wants me to call him by his personal name!*

WHAT'S IT GOING TO BE?

If you see a man sitting on a horse and he is facing the back of the animal, is the man or the horse facing backward?

Were you able to come up with an answer? Most would assume the man is backward, but maybe the horse is backward. In some situations there is clearly one right answer, but sometimes there is more than one.

When it comes to deciding if we want to live by God's ways or our own, the choice seems obvious—unfortunately, we often want it both ways. We want to go along with the crowd that is making bad choices, while we also want to follow what God would want.

When some people wanted to worship both God and an idol named Baal, the prophet Elijah said:

How long will it take you to make up your minds? If the LORD is the one and only God, follow him. But if Baal is the one and only God, follow him.

1 KINGS 18:21 NIrV

Hmmmm, so what's your answer going to be?

147

SAY WHAT?

Question 1: What kinds of animals eat with their tails?

Answer: All animals do—none of them take off their tails to eat.

Question 2: What kind of animal can talk?

Answer: Any animal God chooses to use in that way!

That actually happened. It's recorded in Numbers 22:21–35. God made a donkey speak to his owner Balaam. God sent an angel after Balaam and his donkey to stop them. The donkey saw the angel standing in the road and went off to the side. Balaam beat the donkey but the same thing happened three times. Finally God allowed the donkey to speak! Basically, she said, "What's up, man? You know I don't usually act this way. There's a reason, okay?" (That's the Dr. Devo translation.)

Then God opened Balaam's eyes so he could see the angel. Balaam fell facedown. (And no, the donkey didn't say, "I told you, dude!")

God can use a million ways to try to get our attention. Talk about some of them. Don't forget the clearest ways he has spoken to you.

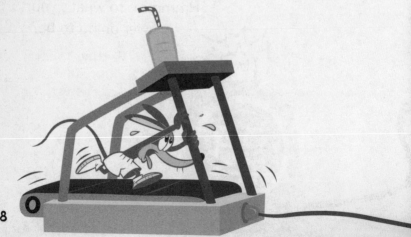

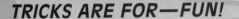

TRICKS ARE FOR—FUN!

Question: What letter comes after *B* in the alphabet?

Answer: *E.*

You may have to think about that one for a while. It's a trick question. Let me write it a different way: What letter comes after *B* in THE ALPHABET?

Sometimes tricks are fun. Sometimes they're silly. And sometimes they're mean. Do you know someone who likes to play tricks on you? Or maybe they like practical jokes?

Before we decide to trick someone or play a practical joke, we need to ask ourselves two important questions: Is it really harmless fun? How would I feel if someone did this to me? Sometimes our need for a good laugh can be at another person's expense.

Enjoy God's gift of fun. Laugh! Tell funny jokes. But think first, remembering:

> Love must be sincere. Hate what is evil; cling to what is good. Be devoted to one another in brotherly love. Honor one another above yourselves.
>
> ROMANS 12:9-10

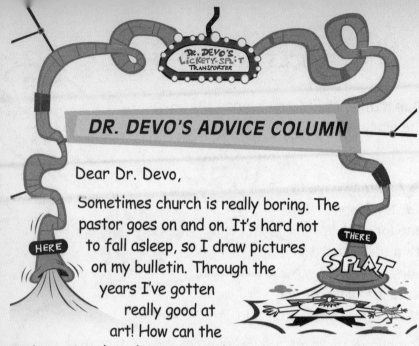

DR. DEVO'S ADVICE COLUMN

Dear Dr. Devo,

Sometimes church is really boring. The pastor goes on and on. It's hard not to fall asleep, so I draw pictures on my bulletin. Through the years I've gotten really good at art! How can the pastor get to be a better preacher?

Signed,

I. M. Bored

Dear I. M. Bored,

First of all, read Acts 20:7–12. You'll get a real kick out of the story about Eutychus. You can relate to him! Secondly, maybe it's not so much the preacher that needs a class in preaching. Maybe you need a lesson in the art of listening. Instead of drawing pictures, take notes. How can you relate the Bible verse he's preaching about to your life? Go to church with an open mind and a positive attitude. And pray that your mind would be open to the Holy Spirit working through the message. Happy listening and learning!

Yawning,

Dr. Devo

DR. DEVO'S ADVICE COLUMN

Dear Dr. Devo,

I'm a pastor. Sometimes I look out while I'm preaching, and it looks like some of the kids could care less about the message I'm sharing. I put a lot of work into preparing the message. I may not be a Billy Graham, but God has called me to be a pastor and I love sharing God's Word. Sometimes it's frustrating.

Signed,

A Shepherd to Bored Sheep

Dear Shepherd,

You have an awesome calling from God. Remember that and don't get in a rut. Don't forget that you are preaching not only to adults but also to kids. Try to give examples that relate to their lives, too. Be creative in your preaching style. Make sure young kids, preteens, and teens feel they are an important part of God's church. Thanks for caring enough about them to write! God bless your powerful and important ministry!

Joy in Jesus,

Dr. Devo

P.S. Is there a preteen in your church named I. M. Bored? If so, maybe you should talk!

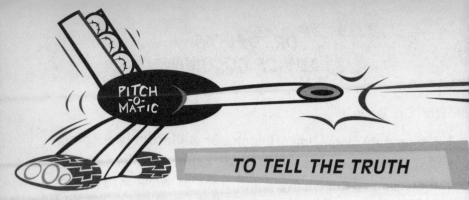

TO TELL THE TRUTH

Question: Why do statues and pictures of George Washington always show him standing?

Answer: Because he wouldn't lie.

Everyone groan! I don't know if the story about George chopping down the cherry tree and not telling a lie to his father is true or not. Someone could be lying about it. Even if George didn't lie about a cherry tree, we can assume that sometime in his life he probably did tell a lie—it could have been a little white one or a great big ol' honker.

Let's see what God says about this subject. I wonder if he will beat around the bush. In the book of Leviticus, God instructs Moses to tell all the people:

> Do not lie. Do not deceive one another.
> LEVITICUS 19:11

That's about as clear as it gets, folks.

Forgive us, Jesus, for the lies we have told in the past, and change us to be truthful, as you are honest and truthful with us. We love you—and that's no lie! Amen.

PRAYER PONDER POINT

Those Expecting Babies

Expecting a baby is a joyful time for a family. But there are always concerns—from the 7,500 diapers to be changed (that's average) to more serious issues!

The months a baby spends in its mother are amazing. Did you know that after two and a half months, the baby's body is completely formed, even its fingerprints? At only three weeks the heart starts beating. Wow!

David praises God in Psalm 139:13, saying:

> You created my inmost being; you knit me together in my mother's womb.

Make a prayer list for those expecting babies as well as for the babies themselves. Here's a starting point.

- ➡ health of baby and mom
- ➡ that mom would get needed rest
- ➡ expectant dads
- ➡ safe delivery
- ➡ that those who can't have children would be able to adopt

PUZZLED?

Ask each person to draw a picture on a piece of paper.

Have fun drawing, and you don't have to stay in the lines!

When you finish drawing, hold the pictures up to show the others. Then tear your picture into pieces. Now have each person pass his or her puzzle pieces to the person on the right. Set a timer or watch the clock for one minute and thirty-seven seconds. See who can put the picture together before the time is up.

Did anyone tear their pieces up really small? Makes it tough, huh?

When bad things happen that tear us into little pieces inside, it can be hard to understand how we will ever feel whole again. We might ask, "Why, God?" But there is one thing we can always be sure of. Though we can't imagine how, God will see to it that the picture of our lives comes back together again.

"My thoughts are not your thoughts, neither are your ways my ways," declares the LORD.

ISAIAH 55:8

BEST FRIENDS

Talk about your answers to these questions. (Don't answer "Jesus" just because you think this is a Christian devotion and that's the right answer! I know how you think!)

Question 1: If anyone you know could be your best friend, who would you choose? Why?

Question 2: If you could have anyone in history as a best friend, who would you choose? Why? (If you did pick Jesus, answer why but also pick someone else and explain your reason.)

How does the following verse match up with your choice of friends?

> Jesus said, "Greater love has no one than this, that he lay down his life for his friends. You are my friends if you do what I command."
>
> JOHN 15:13-14

Say a prayer to Jesus, your friend, for the friends he has blessed you with.

PRAYER PONDER POINT

Laying Hands on Your Hands

Question: Where was Solomon's temple located?

Answer: On the side of his head!

What's between your temples? Your brain! Do you regularly pray for your brain?

Here's an idea you can use in your private prayers. Jesus, the disciples, and other believers "laid hands" on the sick to heal them. They would also do this as a sign of passing on God's Spirit.

> The people brought to Jesus all who had various kinds of sickness, and laying his hands on each one, he healed them.
> LUKE 4:40

I would suggest that you lay your hands on your body when you are praying for yourself. For instance, close your eyes and lay your hands on them. Pray that you will see others as Jesus sees them.

DR. DEVO'S
ADVICE COLUMN

Dear Dr. Devo,

My favorite verse is John 3:16: "God so loved the world that he gave his one and only Son, that whoever believes in him shall not perish but have eternal life." I keep hearing people call that "the gospel in a nutshell." I may be nutty but what does that mean?

Signed,

Confused in a Nutshell

Dear Nutshell Boy,

That's not a nutty question. John 3:16 is sometimes called the gospel in a nutshell because in this one small verse, we learn that God loves us so much that he sent Jesus to die for our sins—the gospel. Now you know! And I'm glad you know the verse and the Savior it talks about. Keep asking questions and—go nuts about Jesus!

Your nutty friend,

Dr. Devo

If you could choose a nickname for yourself, one that everyone would know you by for the rest of your life, what would be your choice? What would you choose for other family members? What would they choose for you? What nickname would your friends choose for you?

These are some of the names that God has chosen for himself. They all describe his relationship with you and me. Check them out!

→ Comforter
→ Lord
→ Mighty God
→ The Good Shepherd
→ Yahweh
→ Messiah
→ Christ
→ Prince of Peace
→ The Vine
→ The Way, the Truth, the Life

Use God's names in prayer and praise to help you understand who he is and what he means to you.

Did anyone pick Dr. Devo's favorite—Immanuel? If you don't know what that name means, check out Matthew 1:23.

FAITH—THE FACTS!

Can you describe what your brain looks like?

Don't know? Maybe that's because you've never seen your brain. Can you describe your spleen? Did you know you had a spleen? What about electricity? Have you ever seen it? Do you believe you have electricity in your home or apartment even though you've never seen it? How do you know?

Faith.

God the Holy Spirit has created faith in you—faith to trust and believe in Jesus Christ as your Savior. Have you ever seen Jesus? How do you know he's real?

Faith.

Hebrews 11 has been called the Faith Chapter. The first verse includes a definition of faith. Fill in the blanks to find the meaning.

Faith is being _____ of what we _____ for and _____ of what we do not _____.
HEBREWS 11:1

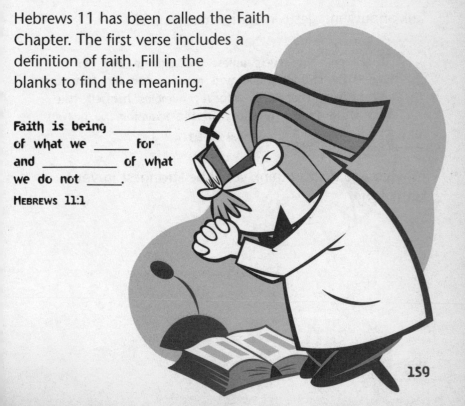

THE YOUNG AND
THE RESTLESS

If you could be any age for the rest of your life, what age would you choose and why?

What would be the good things and what would be the things you wouldn't like about being the following ages?

- ➡ two years old
- ➡ twenty-three years old
- ➡ forty years old
- ➡ sixty-five years old

Talk about what Jesus meant when he said:

> I tell you the truth, unless you change and become like little children, you will never enter the kingdom of heaven. Therefore, whoever humbles himself like this child is the greatest in the kingdom of heaven.
>
> MATTHEW 18:3-4

At what age do you think you'll be strongest in your faith? Why?

STEAL MY HEART, JESUS

Which of the following are examples of stealing?

→ getting an answer from someone else's paper during a test at school

→ making copies of books, videos, CDs, DVDs, or sheet music without permission so you don't have to buy your own copies

→ shoplifting

→ collecting money for a charity but not turning in all the money

→ drinking milk (Is the farmer stealing the cow's milk? What if a cow took your milk?)

Stealing answers for a test, shoplifting, or taking money may be obvious. Did you know that making illegal copies is stealing? How are you stealing from companies, musicians, writers, or others when you make copies without paying for the real thing?

The Bible says:

> Those who have been stealing must never steal again.
>
> EPHESIANS 4:28 NIrV

There is a kind of stealing that is good: when Jesus steals your heart.

Steal my heart, Jesus, and make it yours. Amen.

ARE YOU HAVING CRAB FOR SUPPER?

Question 1: Why is the ocean so grouchy?

Answer: Because it's full of crabs!

Question 2: What lives in the water and takes you any-where you want to go?

Answer: A taxi crab.

There's nothing like a couple of good crab jokes! But there's nothing as bad as a bunch of crabby people! Are you crabby?

Being crabby, mean, and looking at things in a negative way is not God's will for our lives. Paul wrote:

> Be joyful always; pray continually; give thanks in all circumstances, for this is God's will for you in Christ Jesus.
>
> 1 THESSALONIANS 5:16-18

That might sound impossible to do but remember, we trust in the God of impossibilities! When you're having a hard time being joyful, lean on Christ and find your joy in him! Start today by chasing away your frowns with a smile.

We're going to take a time-out for a Dr. Devo spelling test. So come sit for a spell and take (or give) this test:

Correctly spell the following words:

- → devotions
- → giggle
- → computer
- → Galatians
- → fantastic
- → Psalms

Wow, that felt like a quiz at school! Sorry about that!

My point in asking you to take a spelling test has to do with "sitting for a spell." That phrase means "stop for a while, sit down, relax." I would guess that you have some busy days. It's good to stop and take time to relax. But it's even more important that we don't get so busy that we forget about our Lord and his presence in our lives.

Psalm 46 reminds us to sit for a spell and remember that God is in charge. God is here to help. God is with us. Sit for a spell and listen to these words:

> Be still, and know that I am God.
>
> PSALM 46:10

THE LONG AND SHORT OF IT

How long do you think it is from the edge of your fingertip to the top of your shoulder?

If you have a tape measure, take a guess and then note the real length. Then guess the measurement between your outstretched hands, from fingertip to fingertip. Following the guess, use the tape measure across your arms and back to get the real length.

fingertip to shoulder: _____
guess: _____
real measurement: _____
fingertip to fingertip: _____
guess: _____
real measurement: _____

Do you have short arms or long arms? What if God spoke to you today and asked:

Is the LORD's arm too short?
NUMBERS 11:23

That sounds like a weird question, but that's what the Lord asked Moses when Moses doubted God's ability to do something that he'd said he would do.

God wanted Moses to know he could do all things. His arms weren't too short for anything. He could reach the impossible and make it happen! God still can!

GET THE MESSAGE

Here is a funny answering machine message:

Hi! This is Caterina's microwave. Her answering machine ran away with her CD player, so I'm stuck with taking her calls. If you want anything cooked while you leave your message, just hold it up to the phone!"

Some people might think this is kind of foolish, but I thought it was a great message. Paul wrote:

> The message of the cross seems foolish to those who are lost and dying. But it is God's power to us who are being saved.
>
> 1 CORINTHIANS 1:18 NIrV

The message of the cross is that you are forgiven, loved, and saved. When Jesus went to the cross, he took the punishment you and I deserved. To unbelievers that sounds foolish. But as followers of Jesus, we realize that the message of the cross is the way we were saved! That's a message to enjoy hearing over and over again—and to share with others who haven't heard it!

This is kind of a personal question, but I was wondering if your feet smell? Does your nose ever run? Whoa, if your feet smell and your nose runs, I think you might be upside down! I don't know about you, but I run with my feet and smell with my nose!

When Jesus' disciples were arguing about who was the greatest, Jesus stopped them and turned their world upside down. He wanted to turn their thinking upside down. He said:

> If anyone wants to be first, he must be
> the very last, and the servant of all.
>
> MARK 9:35

Wow, that does sound backward and upside down! To be first, we must be last. Who wants to be last? Who wants to serve? Most people don't.

People who give their lives to Jesus aren't concerned about getting the credit. They do things to serve their Savior and others because he serves and loves them. It's fun being in the "upside-down secret service"—serving others without getting the credit. That's the way to live!

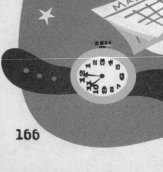

A COOL DEVOTION

Question: What is the coldest letter in the alphabet?

Answer: C—it's always in the middle of ice!

You've probably been in the middle of an icy situation. I'm not talking ice-skating, hockey, or a Popsicle-eating contest. Has anyone ever given you the cold shoulder? Maybe a better question is, Have you ever given someone a cold shoulder?

"Giving the cold shoulder" means to ignore someone—to shut him or her out of a conversation, a group of friends, or an event. That's not cool! If it's happened to you, you know the feeling. If you've done it to others, it's time to ask for forgiveness and warm up your shoulders.

David reminds us that God will never ignore us or our needs in this verse:

> Sing praises to the LORD....
> He does not ignore the cry of the afflicted.
> **PSALM 9:11-12**

(*Afflicted* means those who are hurting.) Thankfully, God will never give us the cold shoulder. He's on our side. That's really cool news!

WATCHA LOOKIN' AT?

You're going to need your parent's permission for this! You might want to go outside. I want to teach you to balance a stick, pole, or broom handle in the palm of your hand. Let's give it a try.

If you try to balance the stick while looking at your hand (where the stick and your palm meet), it won't work. The secret to stick balancing is to keep your eyes focused on the top. That makes all the difference in the world!

You know where I'm heading with this, don't you? Yep, the secret to things going smoothly in your life is to keep your eyes focused on Jesus. The book of Hebrews tells us this:

Let us fix our eyes on Jesus.
HEBREWS 12:2

When we keep looking at ourselves, either we get hurt or we hurt someone else.

Can you think of a story about a disciple who took his eyes off Jesus and things changed quickly? You can read about it in Matthew 14:22–33.

Keeping your eyes on Jesus makes all the difference in the world!

The Homeless

According to the National Coalition for the Homeless, it is estimated that _____ people in the United States are homeless on any given night.

   a. 140,000

   b. 500,000

   c. 760,000

The answer is c.

Add to that the estimate that 1.2 million people experience homelessness during one year! Even Jesus knew what it was like to be homeless. Jesus said:

> Foxes have holes and birds of the air have nests, but the Son of man has no place to lay his head.
>
> MATTHEW 8:20

What are some prayers you could offer up for the homeless? Could you meet any of their needs? Let's make a prayer list.

➡ for shelter and jobs
➡ that shelters would be fully stocked to help homeless children
➡ that their relatives might help
➡ for their mental and spiritual conditions
➡ for volunteers at soup kitchens
➡ that homeless unbelievers might come to know Jesus

A mom was teaching her four-year-old how to unbuckle her car seat. The little girl asked, "Mommy, do I click the square?"

"Yes, honey!" her mom said.

Then the girl asked, "Single click or double click?"

If you could pick one of these computer keys to use in your life, which would it be?

➡ control
➡ escape
➡ home
➡ delete

Depending on the day, I like all those answers! It would be nice to have a delete key for some of the things we say and do. On the computer it's so easy. Point the mouse at the word or phrase to be deleted, drag the cursor over it, and hit delete. Poof! It's gone!

It doesn't seem so easy when we've said or done things that hurt our friends, family, or classmates. But if you've hurt someone, point your life to the cross of Jesus. When you turn away from your sin and toward Christ, he hits delete—a forgiveness key.

Dear Dr. Devo,

I started reading the first chapter of Job. He had everything and then it was all taken from him. But then he says, "The LORD gave and the LORD has taken away; may the name of the LORD be praised" (Job 1:21). How could he praise God at a time like that? My grandma died and I miss her so much. I was mad at God for a long time after she died. How could Job say that?

Signed,

Without a Grandma

Dear Without,

It's okay to miss your grandma. Job missed his family, too! I'm sure he cried, like you probably have. But he decided that while he was sad, he would also trust in God. Job trusted in the resurrection of the dead. Read Job 19:25–26. He trusted that one day he would see his family again. If your grandma believed in Jesus, then she's in heaven. As a believer in Christ, you will spend eternity with her and you won't ever have to say good-bye again!

Praising God with you,

Dr. Devo

FACE - OFF

A SHORT DR. DEVO DEVOTION

Question 1: What man in the Bible has a name that makes him sound very short?

Answer: Nehemiah (Knee-high Miah).

Question 2: Who is a man well known for being short and climbing trees?

Answer: Zacchaeus. Read Luke 19:1–10 for his story.

Zacchaeus was so short, he had to climb a tree to see Jesus. When his Savior wanted to spend the day with him, he came down. A short time after being with Jesus, the man completely changed his ways (Luke 19:8).

The short man realized this truth about himself:

> **All have sinned and fall short of the glory of God.**
> **ROMANS 3:23**

Jesus had come to save him for falling short of God's perfection! Thankfully, Jesus didn't have to save him from falling out of the tree!

FOREVER?
WHATEVER?

A poll showed that ___ percent of people skip ahead to the end when reading a book.

  a. 14

  b. 27

  c. 48

  d. 79

Answer: *b*

At the end of the Bible is a book called Revelation. It's a big book with a lot to say. But one of the things it tells us is that when Jesus returns, we will be together with him forever!

Unlike some other parts of Revelation, that part is pretty easy to understand. But when I was growing up, I was bothered that heaven would go on forever! I just couldn't get my brain around eternity.

That fact doesn't bother me anymore. I realized that the Bible tells us how perfect and wonderful heaven will be. We won't be bothered by time, complaining, "This is taking forever!" We will be happy there. God is so good that forever isn't enough time to praise him for who he is! Read Revelation 1:1–8.

SICK AND TIRED OF BEING SICK AND TIRED

Question: What did one elevator say to the other elevator?

Answer: "I think I'm coming down with something!"

Isn't it a bummer when you're sick? You can't get out and play. You get tired and grumpy. You have to catch up on missed homework.

If you're like the elevator that was coming down with something, look up—to the Great Physician, Jesus. He won't poke around in your ears and nose. When he lived here on earth, he often healed miraculously in an instant. The gospel of Matthew says:

> Jesus went throughout Galilee, teaching ... preaching ... and healing every disease and sickness among the people.
>
> MATTHEW 4:23

Jesus can heal instantly, but many times he uses other means for healing, like poking doctors, bad-tasting medicine, hard-to-swallow pills, operations, tiring therapy, and many other things. Sometimes he heals people by giving them the gift of heaven.

When you are sick and tired of being sick and tired, remember that Jesus won't get sick and tired of helping and healing you—even if you're grumpy!

BOWLED OVER WITH GOOD NEWS

God did not spare his own Son. He gave him up for us all.
ROMANS 8:32 NIrV

If you're a bowler, this Dr. Devo devotion is going to be right up your alley! We'll have a ball looking at this idea that has a fresh spin to it!

When bowlers start a game, the ultimate goal is to score three hundred—a perfect game. But we soon realize that isn't so easy. Even if we get every pin but one, we've messed up.

That's kind of like the Christian life. We want to be perfect but we always mess up.

Thankfully, God comes along and bowls us over with good news. He didn't even spare his own Son. On the cross God gave Jesus the punishment we deserved—death. But he did it so we could be forgiven and saved!

That good news puts us in the tournament of champions, headed up by our risen Savior!

Prayer Warriors

There are many Christians who love spending time in prayer. They are sometimes called prayer warriors. They "go to battle" against the devil, using the power of prayer. Do you know a prayer warrior? Do you know someone who regularly prays for you?

Prayer warriors are like the parable of the widow in Luke 18. That chapter begins with these words:

> Jesus told his disciples ... that they should always pray and not give up.
>
> LUKE 18:1

That's a reminder for all of us. Since prayer warriors spend so much time praying for others, we should pray for them.

Some things we need to pray for regarding prayer warriors include:

➙ giving thanks for them
➙ that they don't give up in their prayers
➙ that their needs are met
➙ that God strengthens their faith
➙ that they continue to find joy in prayer
➙ time for faith, family, and prayer

Thank you, Lord, for all who go to battle with the weapon of prayer! Amen.

DR. DEVO'S ADVICE COLUMN

Dear Dr. Devo,

My name is Duke. I'm a dog. I'm smart and I type. Hey, what else am I going to do while my master is at school? Watch soap operas? I'm fifteen years old. That's ancient in dog years. My master is always talking about Jesus and heaven. I was just wondering if dogs get to go to heaven?

Signed,

Barking Up Your Tree

Dear Barker,

Doggone it, you are a smart dog! And you have a smart master who believes in Jesus. About your question—ummm, well, I don't really know. Here's what I do know: When God created the world, he made animals. (If you can read, check out Genesis 1:24–25.) Jesus came to save sinners. And you don't have a soul to save. On the other hand, when God created perfection in the Garden of Eden, there were animals, so maybe there will be animals when we get to his perfect heaven. That's all I know. Hope it helps.

Bark! Bark! (Translation: Get yourself an extra bone from the cabinet!)

Dr. Devo

Question: What's the difference between a hill and a pill?

Answer: A hill is hard to get up. A pill is hard to get down.

People wonder what's the difference between God—Father, Son, and Holy Spirit—and the gods of other religions. There is only one true God—the God of the Bible who showed the world who he was by sending his Son, Jesus Christ, to live, die, and be raised to life for us.

Jesus is alive—physically and spiritually!

After he rose from the dead, he spent forty days on the earth before returning to heaven. During that time he made sure over five hundred people saw him alive. That way people couldn't say that his body was stolen or that the disciples were making up a story. Check it out for yourselves! Read 1 Corinthians 15:3–8.

All the other gods are dead—most of them weren't even alive in the first place. But Jesus lives! He lives for you and me! That's a mighty big difference.

FOOD FOR THOUGHT

Talk about these Dr. Devo "food for thought" questions.

Question 1: If you could eat only one food for the rest of your life, which food would it be?

Question 2: If all the fast-food restaurants disappeared, how would your life change?

Question 3: If ice cream looked like asparagus (but tasted like ice cream) and cauliflower looked like chocolate cake (but tasted like cauliflower), would that change your mind about eating either food?

Here's some spiritual food for thought. Jesus declared:

> I am the bread of life. He who comes to me will never go hungry, and he who believes in me will never be thirsty.
>
> JOHN 6:35

How do we sometimes treat Jesus like a spiritual fast-food restaurant?

How would things be different if people responded to hearing God's Word in church like they react to being served their favorite food?

God bless your discussion as you "chew the fat" regarding this food for thought!

CAN YOU STAND TO READ THIS DEVOTION?

During what activity do you use the most calories?

a. standing
b. typing
c. driving
d. sitting

Oh, how I wish the answer were *b* and *d*—I'd be in great shape. But the correct answer is *a*—standing. That's not good for me! Most of my time is spent doing *b, c,* and *d!* Maybe I can learn to drive standing up!

Could be I should look at it another way. By standing—standing firm in our faith in Jesus Christ—we may not lose weight, but we can lose the devil. The Bible says:

> Resist [the devil], standing firm in the faith.
>
> 1 PETER 5:9

Stand on the promises of Jesus Christ. Stand on holy ground—God is with you! Stand firmly, in the name of Jesus Christ, and send the devil running away. Stand up for Jesus; don't be ashamed of knowing him.

That's great news! I can't stand the devil, but I can stand tall on the promises of my Savior!

IT'S IN THE GENES

Question: Who invented blue jeans?

a. Levi Strauss
b. Liz Claiborne
c. Tommy Hilfiger
d. Calvin Klein

Answer: *a.* The Strauss family has the original jeans in their genes.

The jeans that you wear are spelled *j–e–a–n–s*. The scientific word that is pronounced the same way is spelled *g–e–n–e–s*.

Genes are a big part of the reason why you look the way you do. They carry the information about your body from your parents down to you. Have you ever been told that you look like one of your parents?

What's really great is if someone says to you, "You have your Father's eyes," and they are referring to you seeing things like your heavenly Father does. What a compliment! What a great faith gene to have inside you. Paul said that Christians are new creations, and we should look at each other in that way.

> From now on we don't look at anyone
> the way the world does.
>
> 2 CORINTHIANS 5:16 NIrV

How does having your Father's eyes change the way you look at others?

181

Which word refers to the point at which a satellite or other object is nearest the planet it is orbiting?

a. perigee

b. apogee

c. aphelion

d. perihelion

The correct answer is a, not "Who cares?"

Don't you love to skip over words you don't understand or can't pronounce? People do that a lot when reading the Bible. There are many words in the Bible that may be easy to pronounce, but since we don't use them in our everyday conversations, we may not know what they mean. Since, as Paul reminds us, the entire Bible is the true, inspired Word of God, we should know what the words used in it mean.

> All Scripture is God-breathed and is useful for teaching, rebuking, correcting and training in righteousness.
>
> 2 TIMOTHY 3:16

With that in mind, Dr. Devo has put together a few definitions of some words found in the Bible.

➡ grace—undeserved love

➡ holy—set apart

➡ doctrine—a teaching

➡ righteous—right, good, innocent

➡ Scripture—the Bible, God's Word

WHAT ARE YOU SO NERVOUS ABOUT?

According to the book *Are You Normal?* by Bernice Kanner, 84.5 percent of us have an annoying nervous habit. Are you one of them?

- → 46.1 percent of us are knee or leg tappers.
- → 44.5 percent of us chew on ice.
- → 4 out of 10 of us crack our knuckles.
- → 27.1 percent of us regularly chew a pen cap or pencil.
- → 38 percent of us peel labels off bottles or cans.
- → 30 percent of us twist or pull our hair.
- → 1 in every 5 of us grinds our teeth.

One hundred percent of us are invited to turn all our worries over to Jesus Christ.

Jesus cares for us all (1 Peter 5:7). It would be a wonderful world if one hundred percent of us cared for others as much as he does! Not only would our teeth, legs, hair, and knuckles appreciate it, but it would also be good for our souls!

DON'T THROW IN THE TOWEL

Did you know that almost half of us claim to change our towels daily or after every shower? That's incredible! A lot of people are throwing in the towel.

The phrase "throwing in the towel" means to give up or quit. Are you a towel thrower? I'm not talking about changing your towels; I'm asking if you tend to give up easily. It can be easy to get frustrated with certain homework assignments, chores, or projects and just throw in the towel.

If you ever feel like throwing in the towel in your walk with Jesus, if things are getting frustrating, check out these great words of encouragement from Paul:

> Forgetting what is behind and straining toward what is ahead, I press on toward the goal to win the prize for which God has called me heavenward in Christ Jesus.
>
> PHILIPPIANS 3:13-14

That should keep you going and going and going, all the way to heaven!

THE MATCH GAME

Match the following jokes with the correct punch line.

____Where do calves eat?

____Where do cows go
for entertainment?

____Where do cattle eat?

a. In re-steer-rants.

b. In calf-eterias.

c. To the moo-vies.

Those might be easy to match. Paul told Timothy:

Continue to follow what you have learned. Don't give up what you are sure of.... You have known the Holy Scriptures ever since you were a little child. They are able to teach you how to be saved by believing in Christ Jesus.

2 TIMOTHY 3:14-15 NIrV

We need to continually study, learn, and even memorize God's Word. Match each passage below with its correct theme.

____Psalm 23

____Ephesians 2:8–9

____Ephesians 6

____Exodus 20

____John 10

____Romans 8:38–39

____1 Corinthians 13

a. The Ten Commandments.

b. The armor of God.

c. The Love Chapter ("Love is . . .").

d. Jesus said, "I am the Good Shepherd."

e. The Lord is my Shepherd.

f. Saved by grace, through faith.

g. Nothing can separate us from the love of God in Jesus.

ARE YOU RESPONSIBLE?

Once when I tried to get a new job, the boss asked me if I was responsible. I told him I was a very responsible person. "In fact," I said, "the last job I had, every time something went wrong, they said I was responsible!"

I didn't get that job! Hmmmm, I wonder why?

Check out Numbers 18:1–7. Aaron and his family were responsible for dealing with the big sacred tent while God's people were in the wilderness. God gave each person a certain responsibility so things would run smoothly.

What kinds of things have your parents, teachers, or God given you to be responsible for? How are you handling it? Okay, now ask your parents for their opinion!

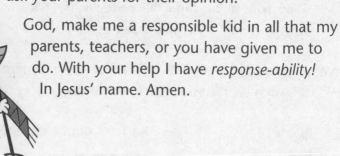

God, make me a responsible kid in all that my parents, teachers, or you have given me to do. With your help I have *response-ability!* In Jesus' name. Amen.

GET IT OUT OF THERE

Define "eclipse." It's not what a gardener does to your bushes. [Think about it!]

An eclipse is when one heavenly body totally or partially blocks another. Sometimes the moon gets between the earth and sun, blocking the sunshine. Then it looks like nighttime—even in the middle of the day.

What is going on in your life that can block your view of the heavenly Son (of God)? How can the following things or people cause an eclipse of the Son?

- ➞ friends
- ➞ shopping
- ➞ TV
- ➞ music
- ➞ self
- ➞ computers
- ➞ sports
- ➞ phones
- ➞ money

Who or what is blocking the Son's light in your life? What will happen if you confess your sins and ask the Son for forgiveness?

> The LORD turns my darkness into light.
> 2 SAMUEL 22:29

Dear Lord, do that in my life! I want to live in the light rather than the darkness. In my life let there be light—your light! Amen!

Check out these signs around town.

Sign on a front door: "Everyone here is a vegetarian except the dog."

Sign at a dry cleaners: "Drop your pants here."

Sign in school near clock: "Time will pass; will you?"

In the Bible the books of Matthew, Mark, Luke, and John tell of signs that show Jesus is truly the Son of God and the world's Savior. He forgave sins, healed people, taught them, drove out demons, died and rose from the dead.

When John wrote the story of Jesus' life, he said:

> Jesus did many other miraculous signs ... which are not recorded in this book. But these are written that you may believe that Jesus is the Christ, the Son of God, and that by believing you may have life in his name.
>
> JOHN 20:30–31

Discuss the different miraculous signs Jesus has shown in your life to remind you that he is your Savior.

Dear Dr. Devo,

I'm not afraid to admit that I'm afraid of those big honker storms with the loud thunder and major-league lightning. I don't know why I am, but I am! Sometimes it even makes me cry. Do you have any ideas that would help me?

Signed,

Stormin' Norman

Dear Stormin',

Everyone has fears. Sometimes those big honker thunder boomers get really loud. Here are a couple of things to remember.

➡ *Thunder is just a noise. There is no way it can hurt you.*
➡ *Since it can't hurt you, just laugh at it.*
➡ *Remember God's promise to always be with you.*

As for the lightning, I would just smile and imagine that God is taking pictures of you beacause He probably wants to keep a picture of you on his desk. God's promise is:

Never will 1 leave you; never will 1 forsake you.

HEBREWS 13:5

Together we're safe in him,

Dr. Devo

HOW DOES IT RATE?

On a scale of 1 to 10 [1 being "boring, needs work" and 10 being "awesome"], rate the following about your church.

worship services	1 2 3 4 5 6 7 8 9 10
messages or sermon	1 2 3 4 5 6 7 8 9 10
ministry to preteens	1 2 3 4 5 6 7 8 9 10
songs or hymns	1 2 3 4 5 6 7 8 9 10
Sunday school /Bible study	1 2 3 4 5 6 7 8 9 10

Rate the following [1 being "So what?" and 10 being "1 believe this is true"].

Exodus 20:8: "Remember the Sabbath day by keeping it holy."

1 2 3 4 5 6 7 8 9 10

Hebrews 10:25: "Let us not give up meeting together, as some are in the habit of doing."

1 2 3 4 5 6 7 8 9 10

I pray you have great worship this week! And I pray you pray about these things today.

Government

Pray for kings.
Pray for all who
are in authority.
Pray that we will
live peaceful
and quiet lives.

1 TIMOTHY 2:2 NIrV

There are lots of prayer ideas in this category that will keep you busy for a while. Here's a starter list that you can add to:

→ that leaders would look to the ultimate Leader

→ the president, vice president, and cabinet members

→ Congress members and their staffs

→ your state government

→ your local government

→ all government workers

→ leaders of other nations

→ members of the military and their families

→ the media that cover government issues

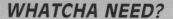

WHATCHA NEED?

Guess who has this motto: "Let me meat your needs!"

a. a vitamin salesperson

b. a vegetable farmer

c. a butcher

Guess who has this as one of his mottoes: "Let me meet your needs!"

a. our Savior

b. our Savior

c. our Savior

The answer for the meaty first question is *c*, and in case you couldn't figure out the answer to the second question, read this:

God will meet all your needs according to his glorious riches in Christ Jesus.

PHILIPPIANS 4:19

What is it you need? (No, not want—need.) Make a list.

_____

_____

_____

_____

How can, has, or will God meet your needs in Jesus? Take time to thank Jesus, your "need meet-er."

VEGGIES VERSUS MEAT

What food best describes your personality?

Since you rolled your eyes at that question, sink your teeth into this one: Would you rather have a meal of vegetables, a meal of the finest meats, just a dry crust of bread, or a big dinner of your choice? (Take time to chew on that for a while before you keep reading.)

Remembering how you answered that last question, stir these two verses into the mix of your conversation:

A meal of vegetables where there is love is better than the finest meat where there is hatred.
PROVERBS 15:17 NIrV

It is better to eat a dry crust of bread in peace and quiet than to eat a big dinner in a house that is full of fighting.
PROVERBS 17:1 NIrV

Come, Lord Jesus, be our guest at our meals and in our house. Replace any anger, hatred, or fighting with your gifts of compassion, love, and peace. Amen.

193

What do you think you will be doing at this exact moment thirty years from now?

- ➡ helping your child with homework
- ➡ coaching a professional arena football team
- ➡ wondering how you got so old so fast
- ➡ loosening your belt and scratching your stomach
- ➡ trying to feed your nine children

These are simple and hope-filled words: We don't know what the future holds, but we know who holds the future. The future scares some people. People like to be in control. Christians can relax and enjoy each day, knowing God holds the future in his hands.

Don't ever get involved with psychics, tarot cards, horoscopes, Ouija boards, and other schemes that Satan likes to use to replace our trust in our Savior. Remember what the Bible says:

> **Since no man knows the future,
> who can tell him what is to come?**
>
> ECCLESIASTES 8:7

Relax! Trust in God! Enjoy his blessings!

IT'S TIME TO GET INTO THE GAME

Some animals decided to play a football game. On the opening kickoff, the rhino charged down the field and scored with eleven animals hanging on to him. Just before halftime, the other team scored and kicked the ball to the rhino's team.

The rhino took the kickoff and started running. But right before the end zone someone tackled him. The players unpiled, and at the bottom was a centipede. His teammates congratulated him for tackling the rhino. One of them asked, "Where have you been? We could have used you earlier!"

The centipede answered, "I was in the locker room—putting on my shoes!"

Take the time to read 1 Corinthians 12:12–31 and talk about how the animal story relates to the story of the body of Christ.

> Now you are the body of Christ,
> and each one of you is a part of it.
> 1 CORINTHIANS 12:27

Are you on the sidelines, in the locker room, on the field, coaching, or in the stands holding or using the gifts God has blessed you with?

Have you noticed that even though the tongue weighs practically nothing, it's surprising how few persons are able to hold it.

Check out this tasty tidbit of wisdom from Proverbs:

> Those who talk a lot are likely to sin.
> But those who control their tongues are wise.
>
> PROVERBS 10:19 NIrV

It's so easy to say something hurtful, to gossip, to yell in anger, or even to use God's name in a sinful way. We can all use our tongues to pray to God to make us wise by controlling what comes out of our mouths (even if it's sticking our tongue out at our brother behind his back)!

Try to take this test before you say something. If what you are about to say doesn't pass, keep your mouth shut!

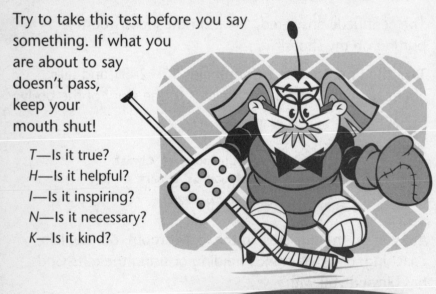

T—Is it true?
H—Is it helpful?
I—Is it inspiring?
N—Is it necessary?
K—Is it kind?

FACE-OFF

DO YOU HAVE
EGG-CELLENT HEARING?

According to the American Egg Board, what color are the earlobes of hens that produce white-shelled eggs?

a. red
b. white
c. blue
d. brown

What color are the earlobes of those that produce brown-shelled eggs?

a. red
b. white
c. blue
d. brown

If you answered *b* for the first question and *a* for the second, you can crow about being correct! Maybe you could get a job as an ear doctor, a chicken farmer, or an egg salesman. Getting back to ears, listen up:

> Listen to his voice today. If you hear it,
> don't be stubborn.... Brothers and sisters,
> make sure that none of you has a sinful heart.
> Do not let an unbelieving heart turn you away
> from the living God.
>
> HEBREWS 3:7-8, 12 NIrV

The invitation to hear God's Word and be saved by it, while turning away from our sin, is for all people!

REWRITE PSALM 23

You may not know much about sheep and shepherding. So how would you rewrite Psalm 23? First read it in your Bible, then fill in the blanks with your own thoughts about the Lord who is your—coach, parent, best friend, teacher, principal, etc.

The LORD is my _____, I shall not _____.
He makes me _____, he leads me
_____, he restores my _____. He guides
me in _____. Even though I
_____, I will fear no evil, for you are with
me; your _____ and your _____, they
_____ me. You prepare _____ before me
in the presence of _____. You _____ my
_____ with _____; My
_____.
Surely _____ and
_____ will follow me
all the days of my life, and I
will_____.

PSALM 23

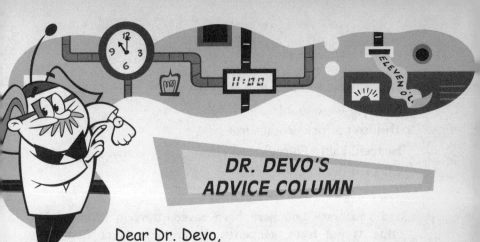

DR. DEVO'S ADVICE COLUMN

Dear Dr. Devo,

I don't like people keeping secrets from me. So why didn't Jesus tell us when he is coming back to take us to heaven? I read in Matthew 24:36 that "no one knows about that day or hour."

Signed,

I Want to Know

Dear Want to Know,

Jesus did promise his disciples (and us) that he would return one day. But he also said, "You should not be concerned about times or dates. The Father has set them by his own authority" (Acts 1:7 NIrv). So take his advice and don't worry about it! Actually, what we all should do is live as though Jesus will be coming back any minute. If you believe in Jesus, you will be judged on Jesus' perfect life, not on your sinfulness. Don't feel bad that God hasn't let you in on the date of his return— no one knows! We're all in the same boat!

Livin' like he's coming back today,

Dr. Devo

Free gift!
Nothing to send in!
This isn't a trick! What's free?
Heaven! Faith! Forgiveness! Love!
Check it out in Ephesians:

It is by grace you have been saved, through faith—and
this is not from yourselves, it is the gift of God—
not by works, so that no one can boast.

EPHESIANS 2:8-9

We can't get those gifts by sending in box tops or being good or doing good things. They are ours but not by any works we do! What incredible gifts! What a Savior!

PRAYER PONDER POINT

Those Who Don't Know Jesus

Jesus wants us to go into all the world and make disciples of all nations (Matthew 28:19–20). As we reach out to others with the good news of the gospel, we can also support other mission fields by praying for unbelievers and those who minister to them.

In a letter to Timothy, Paul wrote:

> I want all of you to pray for everyone.... That is good. It pleases God our Savior. He wants everyone to be saved. He wants them to come to know the truth.
>
> 1 Timothy 2:1, 3-4 NIrV

So what's stopping us? Here's a starter prayer list:

Unbelievers in my—

- family
- school
- town or city
- country
- group of friends
- neighborhood
- state
- world

I'll pray—

- for the words to share with them.
- that they would want to hear what I have to say about Jesus. and my faith.
- for wisdom in when and how to talk to them.
- for confidence.
- for joy in telling.
- for their salvation.
- for their families.

CELEBRATE!

Question 1: If you could invent a holiday, what and when would it be? What would take place on your special day?

Question 2: If you could create a holiday that celebrated something that God has done, what and when would it be? What would take place on this holy day?

We have so much to celebrate! Psalm 145 says:

> I will exalt you, my God the King; I will praise your name for ever and ever.... One generation will commend your works to another.... They will celebrate your abundant goodness and joyfully sing of your righteousness.
>
> PSALM 145:1, 4, 7

Try writing a lickety-split psalm (poem, prayer, song) about God's goodness in your life today. Here's a fill-in-the-blank idea if you'd like some help:

I want to celebrate the goodness of God, my Savior!

Lord, I love the way you _____.

Your promise to _____ *makes me smile.*

I saw your goodness today when _____.

Every day should be a holiday, celebrating _____.

I want to celebrate the goodness of God, my Savior!

OODLES AND DOODLES

Are your notebooks full of doodles? Here are some fun Christian computer doodles.

\o/ \o/ \o/ = praising God!
<>< = fish
(\O/) = angel
0:-) = angel (sideways with halo)

I have always wondered what Jesus was writing or doodling one day when the Pharisees tried to trick him.

> [The Pharisees] were using this question as a trap, in order to have a basis for accusing him. But Jesus bent down and started to write on the ground with his finger.
>
> JOHN 8:6

We have no idea what Jesus wrote in the dirt. Was he pausing to pray or writing a prayer to his Father? We don't know and it really doesn't matter. But there is something about what Jesus did that reminds me he was also human, like us—only without sin. The next time you find yourself doodling, think of Jesus, whose hands wrote in the dirt and were then nailed to the cross. Those are also the hands that wrote our names in heaven's Book of Life.

\o/ \o/ \o/

MAKING PEACE

For this lickety-split devotion, you'll need paper, scissors, and something to write with. Get those materials and come back here lickety-split (but don't run with the scissors)!

Draw a big cross on the paper. Each person cuts a puzzle piece from the paper and holds on to their piece. (Do that now.)

Guess what? You are a *piece* maker! You made a puzzle piece. Congratulations! God's Word has something to say about you:

> **Peacemakers who sow in peace raise a harvest of righteousness.**
> **JAMES 3:18**

Oops! James is talking about someone making peace, not pieces. Never mind. Just put your puzzle pieces back together so they match up. (Do that now.)

Hey, check that out. There's the cross of Jesus. He's the ultimate peacemaker. He made peace between his Father and the world through his death. The verse reminds us to respond to the peace Jesus brought us by being a peacemaker! When we make peace with those around us, we are walking in the ways of Christ.

God's peace be yours, peacemaker!

TIME ON YOUR HANDS

This is from a church newsletter.

The TV is my shepherd, I shall not want.
It makes me to lie down on the sofa.
It tempts me away from the faith. It assaults my soul.
It leads me in the paths of sex and violence for the advertiser's sake.
Yea, though I walk in the shadow of Christian responsibilities, there will be no interruption, for the TV is with me.
It's cable and remote control, they comfort me.
It prepares a commercial before me in the presence of my worldliness.
It anoints my head with selfishness; my coveting runneth over.
Surely laziness and ignorance shall follow me all the days of my life,
And I shall dwell in the house watching TV forever.

The Bible says:

There is a time for everything.
ECCLESIASTES 3:1

How are you spending God's time—the daily twenty-four hours he has given you? How much time do you spend watching TV? If you aren't spending your time wisely, repent and receive God's forgiveness.
Then consider ways you can use it more wisely.

PERSONALIZE IT!

As you rewrite these psalm verses, all you have to do is fill in the blanks with the names of your family. Choose a different name, including your own, for each blank. It personalizes God's Word. You might want to try this with other verses as the Bible comes alive to you!

God is _____'s refuge and strength, an ever-present help in trouble. Therefore _____ will not fear, though the earth give way and the mountains fall into the heart of the sea, though its waters roar and foam and the mountains quake with their surging.

PSALM 46:1-3

The LORD Almighty is with you, _____; the God of Jacob is your fortress, _____.

PSALM 46:11

_____ will sing of the LORD's great love forever; and _____'s mouth will make your faithfulness known through all generations. _____ will declare that your love stands firm forever, that you established your faithfulness in heaven itself.

PSALM 89:1-2

206

Imagine you've switched places with your teacher. Your class is really obnoxious. They aren't listening to anything you're saying. Paper airplanes are flying, while some kids are actually sleeping! What would you do? (Stop and share your answers!)

Being a teacher is a great calling that isn't always easy. Jesus knew that. Even the Pharisees, who kept trying to trick Jesus to get rid of him, called him Teacher.

> The Pharisees went out and laid plans to trap him in his words.... "Teacher," they said, "... Is it right to pay taxes to Caesar or not?"
> MATTHEW 22:15-17

How did Jesus handle those class clowns? He looked them straight in the eyes and told them how it was. He knew their hearts. He answered them and dealt with the situation.

Our Teacher, Jesus, knows our hearts, too. He tells us of our sin but also tells us his good news of forgiveness and love. What a class act! Start your prayers tonight with "Dear Teacher."

BEHIND THE BULLY

Do you know a bully? Maybe you're one yourself.

Read 2 Kings 2:23–25. Wow! That could make a person change his or her ways!

The hurtful words of bullies and the mean things they do can affect a person for life. Have your parents or older brothers or sisters share bullying stories from their lives. Were they the bully or the one being bullied?

Usually kids bully other kids because they are dealing with problems in their own lives. They don't want anyone to know they have a problem, so they bully, hurt, and make fun of others to try to make themselves feel better. But it doesn't work.

Remembering this may help you have compassion for bullies and be able to pray for them. Pray for their hurts, even if you don't know what they are. Instead of returning meanness for meanness, try responding to them in a kind way. Also stand up for those being bullied. Pray. Forgive. Know that Christ's love covers a multitude of sinful words and actions.

A HAIRY DEVOTION

Did you know that for most guys, there are three kinds of hair: parted, unparted, and departed?

Question: What kind of dance do cats go to?

Answer: A hair ball.

Here's some hair trivia. According to the book "Mortal Lessons" by Richard Selzer, the scalp of a young adult has between _____ strands of hair.

   a. 10,000 and 15,000
   b. 100,000 and 150,000
   c. 1,000,000 and 1,500,000

Answer: The correct answer is *b*. That's a lot of hair!

You know what is even more impressive than the number of strands of hair you have on your head? That God knows exactly how many there are.

> Even the very hairs of your head
> are all numbered.
> MATTHEW 10:30

The point of Jesus saying this is that our lives are so important to God that he knows everything about us. And he loves us more than anyone could ever love us.

MONEY TALKS

If you could snap your fingers and have one thing, what would you choose? Be honest!

- **a.** the ability to snap your fingers
- **b.** one million dollars
- **c.** all the video games you want
- **d.** a contract for a professional sports team
- **e.** a million-dollar house
- **f.** the brains to start college next year
- **g.** twenty-five best friends
- **h.** an amazingly strong Christian faith

I'm guessing you didn't pick *h,* yet you know that this is a devotion and that God is listening, so you should answer *h.* Be honest in your choice.

But also think about this verse from the Bible:

> What good is it for you to gain
> the whole world but lose your soul?
>
> MATTHEW 16:26 NIrV

We can have a lot of money, incredible brainpower, fame, or lots of stuff, but if we don't have Jesus Christ as our Savior, we'll lose out on heaven. That's not much of a life, is it?

DON'T BE FOOLED BY A FOOL

Here are some examples of some pretty foolish people.

- ➡ A girl put lipstick on her forehead because she wanted to make up her mind.
- ➡ Did you hear about the guy who tripped over a cordless phone?
- ➡ A man sold his car to get money to pay for gasoline.

It can be dangerous to hang around foolish people. They often want to do things that are wrong. They want you to try things that could be dangerous. Foolish people often don't care about those in authority.

Check out what Proverbs says about hanging around foolish people:

> It is better to meet a bear whose cubs have been stolen than to meet a foolish person who is acting foolishly.
>
> PROVERBS 17:12 NIrV

So watch who your friends are, and spend more time with the best friend you could ever have—Jesus! That's a smart move!

PRAYER PONDER POINT

Thanks for Conveniences

Most of us are pretty spoiled. We have so much. There is so much to give thanks to God for—things we take for granted every day, things that make our lives so easy. The Bible says:

> Is anyone happy? Let him sing songs of praise.
> **JAMES 5:13**

So let's sing and give thanks for all the conveniences we have that make life easier for us. A lot of people don't have these gifts. Keep those people in your prayers, too!

This list is a beginning. Add those conveniences that you are most thankful for:

- cold water
- ovens
- computers
- refrigerators
- airplanes
- telephones
- backpacks
- plenty of clothes
- washers and dryers
- slow-food restaurants
- water heaters
- cars
- showers
- snooze buttons on alarm clocks
- dishwashers
- microwave ovens
- buses
- malls
- fast-food restaurants
- money

A STORY THAT HAS NO END

A little girl came to the beach with her parents. It was her first time to see the ocean. She ran into the hotel, threw on her bathing suit, and headed for the water. She got right up to the waves and stood watching them come in and go out. Her mom came up to her and said, "Isn't it beautiful? Do you want to go in?"

The little girl said, "I think I'll wait for the waves to stop before I go in!"

She's going to be waiting a long time before she ever gets in the ocean.

What else is as constant as, and even longer lasting than, ocean waves? The love of our Lord.

His love endures forever.
PSALM 136:1

Psalm 136 repeats this thought twenty-six times. There is no other love like God's. And he has chosen to share that love with you!

Have a family member read the first half of each verse in Psalm 136. After that is read, the rest of the family can respond, "His love endures forever!"

WHAT'S GOING ON IN YOUR MIND?

A boy asked his mom if she knew what Goliath said when David hit him with a stone.

"I didn't know Goliath said anything," his mom answered.

"Sure he did," the boy told his mom. "David put that stone in his sling and whipped it around and hit big ol' Goliath right between his eyes. Then the giant said, 'Hmmmm, nothing like that has ever entered my mind before.'"

The Bible says:

> Don't live any longer the way this world lives.
> Let your way of thinking be completely changed.
> Then you will be able to test what God wants for you.
>
> ROMANS 12:2 NIrV

A lot of weird, scary, mean, hurtful, and sinful things enter our minds every day, from so many sources that we could never count them. We need to ask the Holy Spirit to change what enters our minds. That will change the way we live.

That's a great thought! Had anything like what that verse said entered your mind before?

MORE DAFFYNITIONS

Here are some more zany daffynitions:

→ detail—what's at the end of de horse
→ belong—to take your time
→ geometry—what the acorn said when it grew up
→ pharmacist—a helper on the farm
→ warehouse—what you ask when you're lost

Now some *real* definitions for Bible words:

→ Christ—Anointed One, set apart for a special task
→ covenant—a treaty, pact, agreement, or contract
→ faith—belief or trust
→ mercy—kindness, sympathy, pity toward undeserving people
→ parable—an earthly story with a heavenly meaning

When you read or hear a word you don't understand, ask someone to explain it. Jesus would explain things to his disciples when they didn't understand what he meant.

With many similar parables Jesus spoke the word to them, as much as they could understand.... When he was alone with his own disciples, he explained everything.

MARK 4:33-34

FACE-OFF

215

Dear Dr. Devo,

In Sunday school we have to memorize Bible verses. What's up with that? I figure it's like any other class in school. I just memorize it for the test and then forget it. I'm guessing that's probably not what I should be doing, huh?

Signed,

What's the Point

Dear What's the Point,

Hey! You already know the answer to your question! Memorizing and then forgetting information after the test isn't a good idea! I hope you will have a desire to know and remember God's Word. Maybe a verse isn't helpful to you right now, but if you have it memorized, it will be there when you need it. Even more importantly, God's Word is one way the Holy Spirit brings you to faith in Jesus and keeps you in that faith. Paul wrote to Timothy, "Do your best to be a peson who pleases God. Be a worker who doesn't need to be ashamed. Teach the message of truth correctly" (2 Timothy 2:15 NIrV). Want to memorize that verse?

Smiles,

Dr. Devo

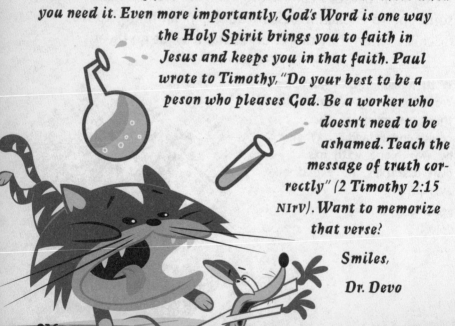

REWRITE
PSALM 100

Psalm 100 is a psalm of thanks. You have lots to be thankful for—how would you rewrite it? First read it in your Bible, and then fill in the blanks with your own words of praise and thanks.

Shout for joy to the Lord, all _____!

Worship the Lord with _____; come before him

with _____; know that the Lord is God.

It is he who made us and we are _____; we

are his _____; the _____ of his

_____. Enter his _____ with thanksgiving and

his _____ with praise; give thanks to him and praise

_____. For the Lord is _____ and

his love _____; his _____ continues

through all _____.

PSALM 100

RUN FOR YOUR LIFE!

A rancher couldn't stop hunters from crossing his pasture until he put this sign up.

It takes sixty seconds to cross this pasture.
My bull can do it in fifty-nine!

That'll get you moving! How fast would you move if you knew the devil was chasing you, trying to get you tangled up with sin? Run for your life, because he's chasing all of us! He can't make us sin, but he loves to chase us, tempt us, and get in the way of our making it to the finish line of heaven. Be glad God is on our running, winning team of forgiven sinners!

Let us throw off everything that stands in our way.
Let us throw off any sin that holds on to us so tightly.
Let us keep on running the race marked out for us.
HEBREWS 12:1 N1rV

Hey, bully Satan, you're in for quite a run. We're on the run for our lives, and Jesus has already defeated you and gives us the victory! Keep on runnin', Dr. Devo readers!

LEARNING FROM THE RUBBER BAND

If you have rubber bands nearby, hand them out and consider these questions.

→ What can you do with a rubber band (good and bad)?
→ What's the purpose of a rubber band?
→ Have you seen different-sized rubber bands?
→ What do you need to know about the strength of one if it's going to be useful?
→ What happens if it doesn't get used and it becomes brittle?

What you can learn from the rubber band (and God's Word)!

→ You can choose to do hurtful or helpful things.
→ Holding things is the purpose of a rubber band. God wants to use us to hold people up, along with his outstretched arms of love and forgiveness.
→ God uses people of all sizes and shapes.
→ Allow your gifts to be stretched so you don't get brittle and break.
→ Know your limits. Know that God has no limits!

You could write "Deuteronomy 13:4" on a thick rubber band, wearing it on your wrist as a reminder to hold on to God's ways.

LET'S (DON'T) GET READY TO RUMBLE!

If your family had seventeen seconds to decide where you wanted to eat supper tomorrow, could you make a decision? What if your family had twenty-three seconds to decide where you would spend your next vacation? How would the decision be made?

That's tough, isn't it? We all have our own ideas and wants. Mix that with the fact that we are often selfish and could easily get into arguments and fights.

When arguments enter your home, here are some things you can do.

- ➡ Pray about the situation. Place it in God's hands.
- ➡ Ask for forgiveness from God and others.
- ➡ Consider God's will in each decision and be open to other ideas.

Keep the following Scripture posted in your home as a reminder of this devotional thought.

> What causes fights and quarrels among you? Don't they come from your desires that battle within you?... Submit yourselves, then, to God. Resist the devil, and he will flee from you.
>
> JAMES 4:1, 7

Peace be with you and your home.

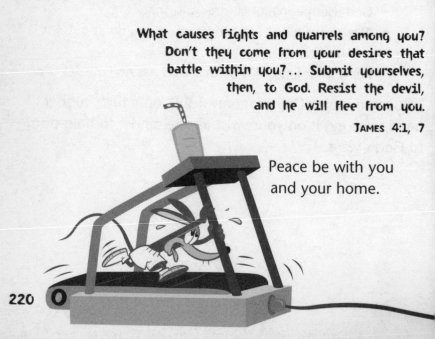

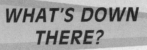

WHAT'S DOWN THERE?

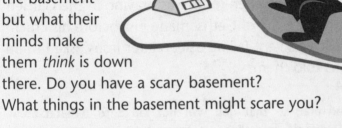

Several kids at a school Dr. Devo visited said that one thing they were scared of was their basement. It's probably not what's actually in the basement but what their minds make them *think* is down there. Do you have a scary basement? What things in the basement might scare you?

a. monsters, gremlins, leprechauns, aliens, or other things your mind makes up

b. spiders and other creepy, crawling bugs

c. weird noises

d. darkness

e. all of the above

Our minds can play tricks on us. Sometimes scary movies, books, or TV shows put bad thoughts in our minds. We need to replace those bad thoughts with a thought like this:

> When I am afraid, I will trust in you.
> PSALM 56:3

That's an easy verse to memorize! Remember it when something makes you scared.

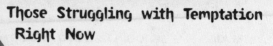

Those Struggling with Temptation Right Now

Question: What happened when the not-so-intelligent camper bought a sleeping bag?

Answer: He spent three weeks trying to wake it up!

When Jesus was praying in the Garden of Gethsemane just before his crucifixion, his disciples kept falling asleep after Jesus asked them to pray. Jesus told them:

> Watch and pray so that you will not fall into temptation. The spirit is willing, but the body is weak.
>
> MATTHEW 26:41

Let's pray this prayer for those struggling with a temptation:

Heavenly Father, we come to you in Jesus' name, praying for people who are struggling with temptation at this very moment. Give them strength to follow your will. Surround their mind and bodies with angels to protect them. Help me when I struggle with temptations. Thank you for the forgiveness you give for all my sins, because of Jesus' death and resurrection. In his holy and strong name I pray as you go to battle for me to fight temptation! Amen.

BEWARE OF . . .

Jenny, a fifth-grader, told me that she is afraid of dogs "that are behind 'Beware of the dog' fences." She probably likes dogs but I know what she means. That "Beware" sign makes us think the dog is awfully scary!

There could be a big, mean dog behind the fence, or the owners could just be trying to scare burglars away.

God tells us that there are some things and some people that we need to beware of. He tells us to beware of the devil, teachers who say they are teaching God's Word but really aren't, and people in the world who don't know Jesus as their Savior.

Jesus said:

If [people] hated me and tried to hurt me,
    they will do the same to you....
    They will treat you like that
because of my name. They do not
    know the One who sent me.

JOHN 15:20-21 NIrV

Beware! But don't be afraid. God is on your side—of the fence!

223

Question: Why was the math book sad?

Answer: Because he had so many problems.

Many kids your age have problems. Some are abused. Some are poor. Others have parents who fight. A preteen wrote this prayer: "Dear Jesus, please be with my parents so they can stay together and I can have a wonderful life. Amen."

It would be great if life were wonderful all the time. But because of sin in the world, it won't be. Prayer is a good place to go for help. Learn to hold on to God's promises that tell you of his great love for you. Are there any mature Christians you can talk to? If you don't know some, pray that God will send someone for you to talk to.

Jesus says to keep thinking about his gift of heaven. Paul encourages us with these words:

What we are suffering now is nothing compared with the glory that will be shown in us.

ROMANS 8:18 NIrV

One day we'll have a perfectly wonderful life!

I THANK GOD FOR YOU AND YOUR FAITH

When I asked some kids your age to tell me about their lives and what they enjoy, I received a paper with these words written by Katie.

I don't like to get up in the morning.
I like to go shopping.
I love to go to church.
I love to read the Bible.
My favorite Bible verse is Revelation 4:8 (part b): "Holy, holy, holy is the Lord God Almighty, who was, and is, and is to come."
I try not to fight with my brothers and sisters (in Christ).
I try not to argue with my parents.
My family tries to help each other.
We all try to get along well.

All I can say, Katie, is the same thing Paul said to the church in Ephesus:

Ever since I heard about your faith in the Lord Jesus and your love for all the saints, I have not stopped giving thanks for you, remembering you in my prayers.

EPHESIANS 1:15–16

HOW WOULD YOU SPEND THE DAY?

If you had the whole day to do anything you wanted to do, how would you spend it? Can you answer right away, or do you need a little time to think about it? When I asked a group of preteens this question, I got some interesting answers.

One girl said that if she had a "hole" day (her spelling, not mine), she would go shopping. Another said she would read. One boy said he would play with his Gameboy. But Lydia's answer was my favorite: "I would walk around and tell jokes!"

That sounds like fun to me! God wants us to enjoy life, to make people smile, and to show we have the joy of the Lord inside our lives. It sounds like Lydia knows what Paul was trying to say when he wrote:

> **Rejoice in the Lord always. I will say it again: Rejoice!**
> **PHILIPPIANS 4:4**

In Lydia's honor, we should end with a joke!

Question: Why is the barn so loud?

Answer: The cows have horns!

SCREENING YOUR EMOTIONS

Here are some computer pictures that represent different emotions. You have to look at them sideways to see the facial expressions. Match the picture with the emotion it represents.

:) _____   **a.** surprised

:o _____   **b.** angry

:D _____   **c.** crying—sad

}o(_____   **d.** smiling—happy

:'(_____   **e.** big grin—very happy

Are you ever afraid to show your emotions? It's okay to cry when you are sad or hurting. But some people don't even like to show that they are happy or enjoying life. What about the fourth picture? It shows anger. Is anger a sin?

Anger is an emotion God has created. It's not a sin (see Ephesians 4:26), but it can easily turn into a sin. That's why a few verses later (Ephesians 4:31) Paul said to get rid of all bitterness, rage, and anger. That's because we often turn our anger into sinful anger with our words or the way we act it out.

Pray to your forgiving God for control when you get angry, realizing it is an emotion—a gift from God—that shouldn't be used in a sinful way.

Our Enemies

You may not like the message of this verse.

> **Love your enemies. Pray for those who hurt you.**
> MATTHEW 5:44 NIrV

Do what? Pray for my enemies? You've got to be kidding!

Jesus wouldn't kid about that. Let's ask the Holy Spirit to make our hearts open to praying for our enemies. When praying for our enemies, it's always best to start by praying for ourselves! Pray that:

→ we would be able to forgive our enemies
→ we would be a good example for them
→ Christian friends would support us
→ we would show Christ's love

Pray for your enemies that:

→ they would forgive you if you have done something to hurt them
→ they wouldn't say or do mean things
→ they wouldn't bully others
→ they would learn to control their temper
→ together we would all learn to live lives pleasing to God

Now let us pray!

EVEN MORE DAFFYNITIONS

Here are a couple more daffynitions for you:

- ➡ carpet—a dog that enjoys riding in an automobile
- ➡ coffee—Snow White's eighth dwarf

Here are some real definitions for Bible or "church" words.

- ➡ Scripture—another name for God's Word, the Bible.
- ➡ Magi—another name for the wise men who visited the baby Jesus.
- ➡ Triune God—*Tri* stands for "three," and *une* comes from the word for "unity." We have one God but there are three persons of God—Father, Son, and Holy Spirit.

After Jesus rose from the dead, he walked and talked with two of his followers on the road to a town called Emmaus. Jesus explained what was said about him in all the Scriptures. After Jesus left, they said to one another:

> He talked with us on the road.
> He opened the Scriptures to us.
> Weren't our hearts burning inside
> us during that time?
>
> LUKE 24:32 NIrV

Pray that you will understand all the words of the Bible so you will grow closer to Jesus.

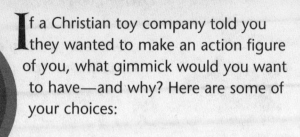

If a Christian toy company told you they wanted to make an action figure of you, what gimmick would you want to have—and why? Here are some of your choices:

➡ the strength of Samson
➡ the wisdom of Solomon
➡ the writing skills of David (complete with pull string)
➡ the blind faith of Paul
➡ the bald head of Elisha
➡ the real tears of Jeremiah
➡ the patience of Job
➡ the hairstyling skills of Delilah
➡ Jonah's ability to stomach anything

God has gifted us each with different talents and abilities. But whatever your skills or whatever super-gifts you wish you had, Isaiah had the right idea. He just stood before the Lord and said:

Here 1 am. Send me!

ISAIAH 6:8

What will be your prayer as you stand before the Lord today?

GETTING TIRED?

Question 1: Why does a bicycle need a kickstand to lean on?

Answer: Because it is two-tired to stand by itself.

Question 2: Why did the boy bury the flashlight?

Answer: Because the batteries were dead!

That boy wasn't too bright—but neither was his flashlight!

Kids never get tired, do they? Kids have a lot of energy but we all get tired, even if we don't want to admit it. It's especially easy to suddenly get tired when we have to do something we don't want to do. I can hear it now: "Clean your room."

"But I'm too tired!"

In his second letter to the Thessalonians, Paul wrote about one thing that we should never get tired of.

> **Brothers and sisters, don't ever get tired of doing the right thing.**
> **2 THESSALONIANS 3:13 NIrV**

That's great advice, Paul. We should have great fun being a Christian and doing what is right. Pray that you never get tired of that!

HOW DO YOU SPELL SUCCESS?

A pantomime is when you act something out without using any sounds. Assign the following Bible story pantomimes to different family members. Since you (the devotion reader) will see the answers, you obviously can't guess, but you can act one out.

➡ the story of Noah's ark
➡ Jesus and Peter walking on water
➡ Jesus feeds the five thousand
➡ the story of Zacchaeus
➡ Jonah's story

Have fun! Come back here when you're finished!

Some people probably found this a tough assignment, and for others it was easy. It's like that with all assignments or jobs. The next time you are doing something, remember this promise from God's Word:

Commit to the LORD everything you do. Then your plans will succeed.
PROVERBS 16:3 NIrV

WHAT'S YOUR FAVORITE FRUIT?

➡ Who in your family likes to put fruit on cereal?

➡ Who likes to eat fruit right off the tree?

➡ What are your two favorite fruits?

➡ Who doesn't like fruit?

The Bible talks a lot about fruit. It says we are to bear fruit—like a fruit tree. Jesus says:

> I am the vine; you are the branches. If a man remains in me and I in him, he will bear much fruit; apart from me you can do nothing.
>
> **John 15:5**

Bearing fruit means that since we are connected to Jesus, we will do things that he would do and speak as he would. Our actions and words will be like the fruit growing on a tree.

What are two of your favorite fruits (good works)? What do you like to do that shows Christ is living in you? Where do you think you bear the most fruit (home, school, with friends, etc.)?

Our fruit gives Jesus the glory as people see him in what we say and do.

Movie, TV, and Radio Studios and Staff

If Jesus came to your house today, what would he think about the TV shows you usually watch, the radio station you listen to, and the last five movies you've seen?

There is some real garbage out there that Satan wants to use to get into our lives. It's a tempting world. But Jesus said:

> **My kingdom is not of this world.**
> JOHN 18:36

We need to be careful about what we watch and listen to. We also need to thank God for good Christian stations and shows. What kinds of things would you add to this prayer list?

→ more Christian movies, videos, radio stations, TV shows
→ writers and actors who will stand up for Christ
→ encouragement for Christian stations and studios
→ that people will buy Christian CDs and tapes to listen to
→ that preteens and teens will not just go along with the crowd

Dear Dr. Devo,

I'm ten years old and my parents treat me like I'm only nine and a half! What can I do?

They hardly ever let me stay home alone. I can only spend so much time on the computer. They even insist on knowing my online password, and they have me on the kid-restricted zone. There are some TV shows they won't let me watch even though all my friends watch them. They make me eat all my veggies. My parents get after me for belching at the dinner table. We never miss going to church or Sunday school.

We even have devotions every night. Tonight we memorized John 13:34: "Jesus said, 'A new command I give you: Love one another. As I have loved you, so you must love one another.'"

And that's another thing—my parents are always telling me they love me.

So, Dr. Devo, my parents treat me, well, umm, like ... they love me ... hmmmm ... very much.

Signed,

Never Mind!

ARMOR ALL—
THE BELT OF TRUTH

In ye ol' days, knights wore suits of armor, and so did the Roman soldiers in New Testament times. But they weren't the same kind. The next few lickety-split devotions are going to take a look at the armor of God that we can wear every day! It's described in Ephesians 6:10–17.

The first piece of God's armor is the belt of truth.

> **Stand firm ... with the belt of truth**
> **buckled around your waist.**
> **EPHESIANS 6:14**

In the time when the apostle Paul lived, people wore tunics, which are like robes. A warrior would put a belt around it so he could move easily and not get caught in his robe. The belt also had a place to hold his sword.

So what's the purpose of a belt of truth? It means truth holds everything together for God's army. We can trust God's Word and promises. He will not lie. We can move easily while fighting Satan's temptations. When Satan tempts us to do something wrong, we can just *belt* him one!

And that's the truth, the whole truth, and nothing but the truth!

ARMOR ALL—THE ARMOR OF GODLINESS ON THE CHEST

Question: Why did the knight run around, shouting for a can opener?

Answer: He had a bee in his suit of armor!

Whew, that sounds painful! But it would be even more painful to have an arrow through your chest or stomach area. Ouch! That's where all your really important organs are! Not-so-minor things like your heart, lungs, liver, stomach, and all those other goodies that keep you alive.

The second piece of God's armor is the breastplate of righteousness.

> Stand firm ... with the breastplate
> of righteousness in place.
> EPHESIANS 6:14

God wants to protect us, and when we always keep him in front of us, he keeps the most important things safe. Things like our faith that the Holy Spirit breathed into us, our heart that pumps his love throughout our lives, and God's forgiveness that gives us hope and peace.

Cover us up with that piece of armor! We need that! We have a lot to protect. Thanks for the armor, Jesus! It fits great!

ARMOR ALL—
THE FOOTWEAR

It's time for Dr. Devo's Roman military trivia.

Caligal are:

a. military gals from California
b. military boots
c. military baby booties

Since the title of this lickety-split devotion is about armor for the feet, the answer is *b*—military boots. A suit of armor is very heavy and uncomfortable. Since that's the case, a warrior had better have something comfy to walk (or run) around in. And boots can't just be comfortable; they also have to protect the warrior's feet.

The third piece of God's armor is the footwear of the gospel (good news) of peace.

> **Stand firm ... with your feet fitted with the readiness that comes from the gospel of peace.**
> **EPHESIANS 6:14-15**

I'm going to let you decide why the Christian warrior needs to put on such footwear! Why do you and your family think Paul mentions this piece of armor? Why are we to wear footwear that is both comfy and protective as we tell others about Jesus and deal with Satan's temptations?

Pray that you'll be comfortable sharing God's peace! Happy talking and I hope you have happy feet!

239

ARMOR ALL—THE SHIELD

The fourth piece of God's armor is the shield of faith.

> Take up the shield of faith, with which you can extinguish all the flaming arrows of the evil one.
>
> EPHESIANS 6:16

One of the most dangerous weapons a Roman soldier had to be protected from was the fiery dart. The head of the darts or arrows were wrapped in material and then soaked in some Roman gunk, called pitch, to help it burn. If a shield made of wood was hit by the arrow darts, it would catch on fire. So good shields had to be covered in hide or soaked in water so they wouldn't catch on fire.

But what about the shield of faith?

Picture your faith—your trust in your Savior Jesus. Picture it as a shield covering you from head to toe. Imagine temptations flying toward you like fiery darts. Your faith in Jesus protects you from the arrows and even puts out the fire.

You're safe, thanks to the faith the Holy Spirit created in you!

ARMOR ALL—
THE HELMET

Heads up! Bombs are dropping out of the sky, trying to destroy you! There's a bomb yelling, "You don't really need Jesus!" Another is screaming, "Believing in Jesus is for nerds!" Incoming! This one has the message, "Don't believe Jesus loves you!"

You'd better have a strong, reliable helmet to protect your mind when Satan tries to drop these bombs into your brain. You need God's helmet of salvation, the fifth piece of God's armor.

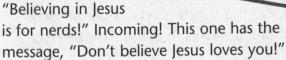

> **Put on the helmet of salvation.**
> EPHESIANS 6:17 NIrV

Dr. Devo knows there weren't bombs when Paul wrote this. But there were temptations and doubts and fears, just like today. The devil wants to get into our heads.

That's why the armor of God includes a dent-proof, lifesaving helmet of salvation. It covers our minds and reminds us that we are saved by the blood and sacrifice of Jesus. Don't fear Satan's attacks. We are covered with the helmet of salvation in Jesus Christ!

ARMOR ALL—THE SWORD

Question: Is the sword an important part of a warrior's armor?

Answer: Well, sword of!

I take that answer back. The sword is very important to a warrior and to all faithful believers. It is the sixth piece of God's armor.

> Take... the sword of the Spirit, which is the word of God.
> EPHESIANS 6:17

A sword is sharp and strong. It can pierce to the core. It can hurt and kill. Just holding it out in front of people can stop them from going forward.

Now it's your turn. Ask your family to help you answer these questions about the sword of the Spirit, which is the Word of God.

How does the Holy Spirit fit in with God's Word?

How does God's Word fit the description of a sword?

Now we've looked at all the parts of the armor of God. Do you remember them? Have you been thinking about your suit of armor lately? So what do you clink—I mean, think? Does the armor of God fit you perfectly or what?

PRAYER PONDER POINT

Praying in Armor

Read Ephesians 6:10–17 as a review about the armor of God.

After Paul wrote about the armor of God, he told us to pray.

At all times, pray by the power of the Spirit. Pray all kinds of prayers. Be watchful, so that you can pray. Always keep on praying for all of God's people. Pray also for me. Pray that when I open my mouth, the right words will be given to me. Then I can be bold as I tell the mystery of the good news.

EPHESIANS 6:18-19 NIrV

Take time now to follow Paul's words and pray.

→ Pray all kinds of prayers (sing a prayer, hum a prayer, read a prayer, recite a prayer by memory, etc.).

→ Ask God's Spirit to give you things and people to pray for.

→ Pray about wearing the armor of God and for safety from temptation.

→ Pray for specific people who may need God to give them the right words today as they share the good news of Jesus.

SING, SING, SING SOME SONGS

I read in Psalm 40:3 that the Lord put a new song in the psalmist's mouth. It was a hymn of praise to our God. Cool, huh?

Recently I was wondering what songs we all know that would describe some of the people in the Bible (with some minor changes).

These are the ones I came up with:

➡ Noah's favorite: "Row, Row, Row Your Ark" (Genesis 6–9)
➡ Samuel's favorite: "Do You Hear What I Hear?" (1 Samuel 3:1–18)
➡ The favorite of Pharaoh's daughter: "What Child Is This?" (Exodus 2:1–10)
➡ David and Jonathon's favorite: "Friends" (1 Samuel 20)
➡ Job's favorite: all the music from "The Wizard of Uz" (Job 1:1)
➡ Paul and Silas's favorite in prison: "Jailhouse Rock" (Acts 16:22–36)

Can you add any others to these? I also figured Jesus liked "light" music (John 8:12), Peter liked hard rock (Matthew 16:17–18), and Methuselah liked the oldies (Genesis 5:27).

I pray that God puts a new song in your mouth today!

ROLL MODEL OR ROLE MODEL?

Do you have a role model? A hero? Someone you look up to?

Sometimes kids choose sports figures as role models. There are some very good, Christian role models in the sporting world. But there are some I wonder about. Check out these interesting quotes from sports figures, who will remain nameless.

→ A former football player said, "Nobody in football should be called a genius. A genius is a guy like Norman Einstein."

→ A senior basketball player at the University of Pittsburgh said, "I'm going to graduate on time, no matter how long it takes."

→ A hockey player explained why he keeps a picture of himself on his locker. He said, "That's so when I forget how to spell my name, I can still find my clothes."

I don't know about you, but I think I'll make Jesus my hero. He says life-changing things like:

God so loved the world that he gave his one and only Son, that whoever believes in him shall not perish but have eternal life.

JOHN 3:16

ALL I REALLY NEED TO KNOW I LEARNED IN SUNDAY SCHOOL

Robert Fulghum wrote *All I Ever Needed to Know I Learned in Kindergarten*. It's a wonderful piece of writing but here's my version. It's called *Most of What I Really Needed to Know About Life I Learned in My Sunday School Kindergarten Class.* These are some of the things I learned.

- Share everything you've learned.
- Live the lessons.
- Pray continually.
- Love the Lord your God with all your heart, soul, mind, and strength, and love your neighbor as yourself.
- Repent and receive God's forgiveness.
- Seek first God's kingdom.

Remember the story in the Bible about the cross, Jesus' death, and his Resurrection? Everything you need to know is in that story.

Imagine what a better world it would be if we all had donut holes and Red Sea punch while singing "Jesus Loves Me," and if every family would thank the Master Teacher.

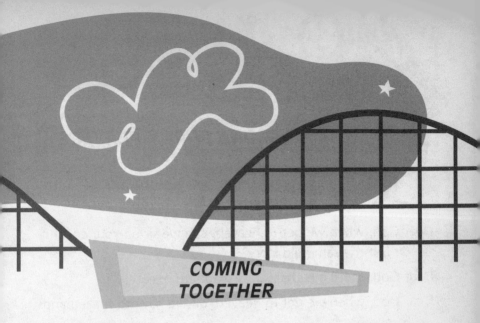

COMING TOGETHER

Sometimes two or three companies come together to form one company. This is called a merger. When that happens, they often use parts of their old company names to form a name for the new company. Let's bring some real companies together and consider what they might be called:

- ➡ If Denison Mines merged with Alliance and Metal Mining, they might be called Mine, All Mine.
- ➡ If Grey Poupon merged with Dockers Pants, they might be called Grey Poupon Pants.
- ➡ If Upjohn merged with Chuck E. Cheese Pizza, they might be called, Upchuck!

One group that did come together and saw great things happen were those who became believers just after Pentecost. Over three thousand people were baptized that day.

> The believers studied what the apostles taught.
> They shared life together. They broke bread and ate together.
> And they prayed. Everyone felt that God was near.
>
> ACTS 2:42-43 NIrV

God and his people—what a great merger!

DOGGONE FUNNY PRAYERS

I found these "prayers from dogs" on an Internet humor page.

Dear God, when we get to heaven, can we sit on your couch? Or is it the same old story?

Dear God, more meatballs, less spaghetti, please!

Dear God, when we get to heaven, do we have to shake hands to get in?

Dear God, are there dogs on other planets or are we alone? I have been howling at the moon and stars for a long time, but all I ever hear back is the beagle across the street.

Dear God, are there mailmen in heaven? If so, will I have to apologize?

Dear God, when my family eats dinner, they always bless their food but they never bless mine. So I've been wagging my tail extra fast when they fill my bowl. Maybe they'll get the hint!

All I can say after those is:

Let everything that has breath praise the LORD.
PSALM 150:6

(Even if "everything" includes dogs with bad breath!)

DR. DEVO'S ADVICE COLUMN

Dr. Devo,

I'm twelve years old and I want to get plastic surgery. My nose is too big. People are always looking at it. I'm enclosing a picture. What do you think?

Signed,

Nosey

P.S. My brother has a question about his nose: is it okay for him to pick it?

Dear Nosey,

Tell your brother, "Only if it goes on strike!" (Have your parents explain that!)

Thanks for the picture. God has made you beautiful. You may think everyone is looking at your nose, but I have a feeling they are just looking into your eyes and you're imagining they're checking out your nose. You "nose" what I mean?

David wrote in Psalm 119:73, "Your hands made me and formed me."

God didn't make a mistake when he created your nose. You seem to be telling God he goofed up. God made you beautiful. Thank him for who you are!

Dr. Devo

OOPS!

Here are some bloopers from church bulletins. (This might be a good time to pray for your church secretary!)

> The music director invites any member of the congregation who enjoys sinning to join the choir.
>
> Weight Watchers will meet at 7:00 p.m. at First Community Church. Please use the large double doors at the side entrance.
>
> Today's sermon: "Jesus Walks on the Water." Tonight's sermon: "Searching for Jesus."
>
> This afternoon there will be a meeting in the south and north ends of the church. Children will be baptized at both ends.
>
> Thursday night—potluck supper! Prayer and medication to follow!

Oops! Here's a message with no mistakes:

Everyone has sinned. No one measures up to God's glory. The free gift of God's grace makes all of us right with him. Christ Jesus paid the price to set us free.

ROMANS 3:23-24 NIrV

Thankfully, God forgives all our mistakes!

LICKITY-SPLIT BIBLE ROUNDUP

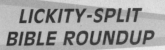

Talk about a lickety-split devotion. Someone decided they could summarize the Bible in less than fifty words! Check this out.

God made.	Saul freaked.
Adam bit.	David peeked.
Noah arked.	Prophets warned.
Abraham split.	Jesus born.
Joseph ruled.	God walked.
Jacob fooled.	Love talked.
Bush talked.	Anger crucified.
Moses balked.	Jesus died.
Pharaoh plagued.	Love rose.
People walked.	Spirit flamed.
Sea divided.	Word spread.
Tablets guided.	God remained.

Lickety-split, short and sweet. God remains with us. No matter how short and fast our days, Jesus has promised:

I am with you always, to the very end of the age.
MATTHEW 28:20

251

MORE COUNTRYSIDE PRAYERS

Fill in the blanks with countries to complete the sentences. [Answers are below.]

1. Little Miss Muffet liked neither curds _____.

2. The sun will come up when it comes up. You can't _____ sunrise.

3. You're acting weird. What's gotten _____?

4. I see your sister is doing your homework for you. _____ do it?

5. I don't like coffee but I really _____.

6. _____ guess the answer to this one?

Jesus said:

Go and make disciples of all nations, baptizing them in the name of the Father and of the Son and of the Holy Spirit, and teaching them to obey everything I have commanded you.

MATTHEW 28:19-20

Pray for the countries above so their people will know Jesus as their Savior from sin, death, and the Devil. Include pastors; missionaries; those being persecuted because of their Christian faith; families; and the leaders of the countries.

7. Remember, people are _____ for God's love!

Answers: 1-Norway, 2-Russia, 3-India , 4-Jamaica, 5-Haiti, 6-Kenya, 7-Hungary.

CROSS-WORDS

Not everyone enjoys crossword puzzles. Not everyone likes to hear words about the cross of Jesus, either. Paul wrote:

Many live as enemies of the cross of Christ.
PHILIPPIANS 3:18

But we want to keep the cross before us. It is a constant reminder of our salvation through Jesus.

Write the word *cross* six times on a piece of paper, leaving plenty of space around it. Use that as the "across" word in a two-word crossword puzzle. Using the *o* in *cross* as the connecting link to the clues below, complete these cross-words.

1. without hope (*o* is the second letter)
2. feeling alone (*o* is the second letter)
3. thinking poorly of yourself (two words—*o* is the second letter)
4. feeling down; filled with gloom (*o* is the third letter)
5. feeling burdened; worried (*o* is the third letter)
6. opposite of found (*o* is the second letter)

How can the message of Jesus and his cross change the "down" feelings and situations? Visit the cross in prayer tonight.

Answers: 1-hopeless, 2-lonely, 3-low self-esteem, 4-gloomy, 5-troubled, 6-lost.

BODY LANGUAGE

Using the clues below, name the appropriate body part.

1. grown on a cornstalk: _____
2. tropical trees: _____
3. parts of a clock: _____ and _____
4. branches of a tree: _____
5. a clam: _____
6. a type of watch: _____
7. a student: _____

Our bodies are living miracles. Blood is pumping. Nerves are nerving. Parts are moving. Eyes are seeing. Our brains are thinking (well, sometimes). Muscles are flexing. Eyelids are blinking. Hair is growing. Noses are smelling. And I'm going to guess that your mouth is looking forward to praying for and giving thanks to your Creator for different body parts he has blessed you with. Let's not take our miraculous bodies for granted.

Your hands made me and formed me.
PSALM 119:73

Answers: 1-ears, 2-palms, 3-face and hands, 4-limbs, 5-muscle, 6-wrist, 7-pupil.

HIGHS AND LOWS

How much time do you and your family spend talking to each other? Is your answer, "Not much; too busy"? If so, have no fear! Dr. Devo's lickety-split family communication kit can help! The kit contains two simple questions you can ask each other every day. They are:

1. What was the low point of your day?

2. What was the high point of your day?

(Note: For variety you can switch the order of the questions!)

David wrote:

> Even though I walk through the valley of the shadow of death, I will fear no evil, for you are with me.
>
> **PSALM 23:4**

A valley is a low point. God is with us even in our lowest valleys. We don't have to be afraid. Isn't God good!

If you have time to spare, have everyone pick some of the high and low points of Jesus' life. Was the valley of the shadow of his death a low point or a high one? That should get you talking—to each other and to him!

Eight- to Twelve-Year-Olds

I know what you're thinking—There's not much written on this page. That's true. And that means you're going to have to fill in the blanks! As you spend time in prayer for kids who are preteens, ages eight to twelve, decide what and who you need to pray for. And parents of preteens, you get to throw in your ideas, too—we want to pray for you. What are your needs? The prayer thoughts are divided into three groupings. What are your personal prayer requests? Then pray for specific needs of classmates, friends, or preteen relatives. And don't forget the parents' requests!

My personal prayer requests:

My prayer requests for classmates, friends, and relatives who are preteens:

My parents' prayer requests:

> 1 want all of you to pray for everyone.
> Ask God to bless them. Give thanks for them.
>
> 1 Timothy 2:1 NIrV

I wish people wouldn't call memorizing Bible passages "memory work"! That makes it sound like it isn't fun or worthwhile. I like what the psalmist wrote:

> I have hidden your word in my heart
> that I might not sin against you.
> **PSALM 119:11**

There are many reasons to memorize, or hide in our hearts, God's Word.

→ It gives us strength to say, "No!" to temptation.
→ It can make us feel better when we are feeling sad.
→ It can remind us that we are loved when we feel alone.

Here are some other passages you might want to memorize. Pick one to hide in your heart and mind! Happy hiding!

→ Psalm 46:1: "God is our refuge and strength, an ever-present help in trouble."
→ Philippians 4:13: "I can do everything through him who gives me strength."
→ John 14:27: "Jesus said, 'Peace I leave with you; my peace I give you.'"
→ Psalm 119:105: "Your word is a lamp to my feet and a light for my path."

WHAT'S YOUR FAVORITE BRAND?

Does your family ever eat off-brand foods? They aren't the popular name brands that everyone knows—they're similar but cheaper. They come in plain white boxes or bags with nothing more than "sugar" or whatever printed on them.

Do you ever feel like a no-name kind of kid? Or it could be you're not so popular and you don't have fancy packaging like some other kids your age.

If that's the case, I want you to know that God has created you to be very special. And he has put his name on you! What an honor! You are God's child. You are a Christian— Christ's name is part of yours.

God has called you by name and "branded" you with his name. You belong to him—the King of Kings, the Creator of the universe, the world's Savior.

> Know that the Lord is God.
> It is he who made us, and we are his.
>
> PSALM 100:3

THE SEVEN WONDERS OF THE WORLD

There are a couple of different lists of "wonders" of the world. One is a list of seven amazing things humans have made, including the pyramids of Egypt and a temple in Greece. Another is a list of seven things that God has made. (They are actually called the Seven Natural Wonders of the World.) That list includes the Grand Canyon, Mount Everest, Victoria Falls in Africa, the Great Barrier Reef, and others.

Now it's your turn to make a list. What seven wonders would you choose? Are they man-made or God-made? Have you seen these wonders? Sometimes it's easy to consider what humans make and give them all the credit, forgetting that God has blessed them with the talent and ability to do it. And other times we take for granted all the wonders God created.

Your List of the Seven Wonders of the World:

1. _____
2. _____
3. _____
4. _____
5. _____
6. _____
7. _____

The earth is the LORD's,
and everything in it, the world,
and all who live in it.

PSALM 24:1

259

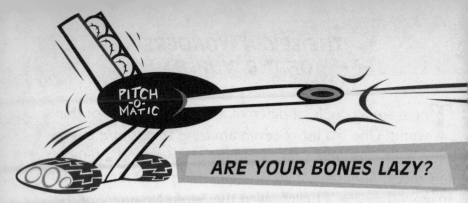

ARE YOUR BONES LAZY?

Question: Why did the lazy man want a job in a bakery?

Answer: So he could loaf around!

It is so easy to be lazy! Our beds are so warm. The sofa is so comfy. The TV is so entertaining. Video games are meant to be played for hours. Computer games and the Internet are so good at sucking us into the screen.

Here's something God says in his Word about laziness:

> Hands that don't want to work make you poor.
> But hands that work hard bring wealth to you.
>
> **PROVERBS 10:4 NIrV**

- ➡ Laziness at home leads to laziness at school.
- ➡ Laziness at school affects our laziness in friendships.
- ➡ Laziness with people leads to laziness in our relationship with Jesus.

It leads to laziness in our faith. You know what I mean:

"Ah, we don't need to go to church every week. Let's sleep in."

"Devotions again? And aren't we praying too much?"

It's so easy to be lazy. But it can be so much more fun serving God and others because Jesus first served us.

WATER WORKS

Question 1: What happens when you throw a green stone in the Red Sea?

Answer: It gets wet!

Question 2: What runs but never walks?

Answer: Water!

Question 3: What's your favorite water story? (You must provide the answer.)

Water can be a lot of fun! Sprinklers, pools, rivers, lakes, hoses, water balloons, washing cars, rain, baptism, and so much more! Baptism? Fun? Listen to these words:

> Don't you know that all of us who were baptized into Christ Jesus were baptized into his death? We were therefore buried with him through baptism into death in order that, just as Christ was raised from the dead through the glory of the Father, we too may live a new life. If we have been united with him like this in his death, we will certainly also be united with him in his resurrection.
>
> ROMANS 6:3-5

Wow! What fun, exciting, life-changing news!

SLEEP LOOSE

Sleep tight! Lots of people say that to someone before they go to bed. Years ago many beds had ropes under the mattresses instead of boards or metal pieces. They didn't want to sink into a loose mattress, so they would tighten the ropes and then say, "Sleep tight!"

Sleep tight? Hey, the ropes are gone from our mattresses! Let's get rid of the phrase and start a new one! When we say, "Sleep tight" to someone, it sounds like we're hoping they will go to sleep all tight, worried, afraid, and nervous. Who wants to sleep like that?

Let's make a change! From now on let's say, "Sleep loose!" Relax, don't worry, give everything to Jesus, don't be afraid, sleep peacefully—in other words, sleep loose!

I even think Jesus would like this new bedtime tradition, because he told people:

> I tell you, do not worry.
> MATTHEW 6:25

Relax! Sweet snoozes! Don't worry! Go to sleep with a smile! Happy zzzzzzzz's to you!

Nice nappin'! Rest rocks! Sleep loose!

WILL I GET A GOOD GRADE?

Question: Why is Alabama the smartest state in the U.S.A.?

Answer: Because it has four *A*'s and one *B*!

Grades make some kids nervous. How nervous would you be if God gave grades? Take turns talking about what grades you deserve for this year in the following subjects.

_____prayer
_____worship
_____telling others about Jesus
_____offerings (tithing)
_____reading the Bible
_____personal or family devotions
_____forgiving others

I bet that wasn't very much fun! It probably wasn't very easy either!

Sometimes we think God grades us on what we do, and we get all worried and uptight. We start avoiding him because we're embarrassed or we think he's mad at us. Thankfully, it doesn't work that way. Here's what Paul told us:

God has shown us how to become right with him.... It has nothing to do with obeying the law. We are made right with God by putting our faith in Jesus Christ. That happens to all who believe.

ROMANS 3:21-22 NIrV

WHO CAN MAKE THE LOUDEST NOISE?

The time has finally arrived—Dr. Devo's lickety-split "Who can make the loudest noise?" contest! Everyone in your house is a contestant. First, here are the rules:

➡ Participants must be under the age of 109.
➡ You can only make noise for seventeen seconds.
➡ To make noise, you can only use your own body parts.
➡ The winner is decided by family vote.
➡ Extra points given for creativity.

Wow! That was *loud!*

Now think about this: The Bible, especially the Psalms, includes many verses about singing loudly, shouting, and making a glad noise. But each verse says the noise, the loud songs, and the shouting should be done in praise to God.

Make a joyful noise to the Lord who has forgiven and saved you!

Shout with joy to God, all the earth!
Sing the glory of his name;
make his praise glorious!

PSALM 66:1-2

LISTEN UP!

A teacher asked a student, "Are you having trouble hearing? You don't seem to be paying attention."

The student responded, "I'm not having trouble hearing—I'm having trouble listening!"

Are you a good listener? What would your parents say about that? How about your teachers?

"Huh? Were you talking to me? What?" (Does that sound like you?)

Read 1 Samuel 3:1–10. You may want to read it like a drama. Four voices are needed: Narrator, Eli, Samuel, and the Lord. Then try to answer these questions.

- What's the difference between hearing and listening?
- How does the Lord talk to us today?
- How could your days be different if you started out by saying what Samuel said to the Lord?

Speak, for your servant is listening.

1 Samuel 3:10

- Do you think you'd really spend time listening for the Lord speak to you during the day?

Spend the next seventy-two seconds being quiet and listening.

EVER FEEL INVISIBLE?

Patient: Doctor, Doctor, I keep thinking I'm invisible.

Doctor: Who said that?

It's the pits when you have something to say and it's like everyone is ignoring you. Hello! I'm here! I have something to say! Does anyone care?

Have everyone in your family share a time when they felt invisible—a time when it seemed no one cared. Go ahead and do that now. I'll take notes with my Dr. Devo invisible ink pen!

So what can we do about those feelings? Maybe some forgiveness needs to be shared. We can also remember that what is really important is how God sees us.

Check out this visible good news:

> How great is the love the Father has given us so freely! Now we can be called children of God. And that's what we really are! The world doesn't know us because it didn't know him.
>
> 1 JOHN 3:1 NIrV

Your heavenly Father sees you. You're never invisible to him!

ARE YOU PROUD OF YOUR HUMILITY?

If you have a dictionary, look up pride, proud, humility, and humble. When you find their definitions, read them out loud. If you don't have a dictionary, quick, run to the store and get one! Wait! I was joking. Talk about what those words mean to you. (Go ahead. I'm waiting!)

Here are some lickety-split questions for your family to talk about.

1. Do you think you are prideful or humble or somewhere in between?
2. Are there times when being proud of someone or something is okay?
3. What are some ways you can be humble in your life? (And no, you're not bragging by answering this!)
4. Is it possible to be proud of your humility?

Talk about what the following verse means. Then have a prayer together.

> When pride comes, shame follows. But wisdom comes to those who are not proud.
>
> PROVERBS 11:2 NIrV

MEMORIES!

Patient: Doctor, Doctor, I've lost my memory!

Doctor: When did this happen?

Patient: When did what happen?

Does this sound like a conversation in your house?

Mom: "I told you to clean up your room."

You: "I forgot."

Dad: "You were going to call Grandma last night."

You: "I remember that I said I would, but I forgot to do it."

Could this be a conversation between you and God?

You: "LORD, remember your great mercy and love" (Psalm 25:6 NIrV).

God: "I will never forget."

You: "Don't remember the sins I committed when I was young" (Psalm 25:7 NIrV).

God: "I forgive you and I will forget your sins."

You: "Remember me because you love me. LORD, you are good" (Psalm 25:7 NIrV).

God: "I do love you and I hope you will never forget my love for you."

How can God's conversation with you change your forgetfulness and the conversations you have with your parents? Remember, God will never forget you.

IS THERE TIME FOR EVERYTHING?

The next few devotions are based on verses from Ecclesiastes 3:1–8.

The first verse is:

> There is a time for everything.
> There's a time for everything that is done on earth.
>
> ECCLESIASTES 3:1 NIrV

Make a list of how you spent the last twenty-four hours. The categories include:

- → sleeping
- → playing
- → eating
- → TV, computer, video games
- → school, homework, reading
- → God, faith-related things
- → chores, working
- → goofing around

Now ask yourself these questions.

1. Were there other things you wanted to do but ran out of time?
2. Why didn't you have enough time?
3. Was that your fault? Or was it God's fault?
4. How could you make better use of your time?
5. When are you going to make those changes?
6. What help can you get from your family?

By the way, if you have time on your hands, be sure to spend some of it on your knees— in prayer!

There is a time for everything. There's a time for everything that is done on earth. There is a time to be born. And there's a time to die. There is a time to plant. And there's a time to pull up what is planted.

ECCLESIASTES 3:1-2 NIrV

If you have a birth story or a death story to share, take time to do that now.

Discuss the questions you may have about being born or dying. If you don't know the answers, take time to ask someone who might know.

Why is there pain in coming into this world? And why is there pain in leaving this world? (The answer is in Genesis 2:16–17 and 3:1–19.)

Besides the birth and death of people, what other things are being born or dying every day? What things are coming and what things are going?

Close with a prayer thanking God for your birth story and Jesus' birth story. Pray about those who may be dying and thank Jesus for his death (and Resurrection) story.

A TIME FOR— LOVE AND HATE

There is a time for everything. There's a time for everything that is done on earth.... There is a time to love. And there's a time to hate. There is a time for war. And there's a time for peace.

ECCLESIASTES 3:1, 8 NIrV

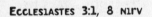

Jesus tells us to love him and to love our neighbor as ourselves. He even says to love our enemies. If we love even our enemies, what is left to hate?

Amos 5:15 reads, "Hate evil, love good." Psalm 97:10 says, "Let those who love the LORD hate evil." Proverbs 8:13 NIrV is similar: "To have respect for the LORD is to hate evil." There's your answer.

Then there are the times of peace, which we love. Times of peace that only the Lord can give. But we are also in a war every day with Satan. Thankfully, God the Victor is on our side!

Love all.

Hate evil.

Enjoy peace.

We are his victorious soldiers!

LIGHTS! ACTION!

Moths and bugs love light! What's with that? I'm glad I'm not a bug! My eyes would be buggin' out because of the light!

Bugs probably spend more time hanging around lights than we spend hanging around the Light of the World! We should spend all our time right next to the Light. If we would do that, our eyes of faith would be improved. We would start to see ways to help others, ways to bring other kids to the Light, ways to forgive, ways not to be mean (even to the bullies).

God is light. There is no darkness in him at all. Suppose we say that we share life with God but still walk in the darkness. Then we are lying. We are not living by the truth. But suppose we walk in the light, just as he is in the light. Then we share life with one another. And the blood of Jesus, his Son, makes us pure from all sin.

1 John 1:5-7 NIrV

(There's more "light" reading in Psalm 27:1 and Isaiah 60:1-2.)

What if you could be either the best-looking, the most athletic, the most musically talented, or the smartest kid in your class or neighborhood? Which would you choose?

Is that a tough question? Let me make it tougher. What if I asked you the same question but added one more thing to choose from: the most faithful (to Jesus Christ)?

As a preteen, it might be hard to think about wanting to have the strongest faith in your class or neighborhood. You believe in Jesus, right? So that's not as big a deal as being the best athlete or being the smartest or things like that. Right? Wrong!

No matter our age, God wants us to continue to grow closer and closer to him. He wants to be first in our lives. He wants us to be faithful to him, to trust him, whatever our age. It's so important. Pray about asking God to strengthen your faith. If that's what you decide to do, you're one smart (and blessed) kid!

WHY DOES GOD NEED MONEY?

One Sunday a pastor told the congregation, "I have good news and bad news. The good news is, we have enough money to start our food pantry, build new Sunday school rooms, and support a missionary in Brazil. The bad news is that it's still out there in your pockets!"

God could get a lot done if we'd let him use "his" money! But we like to keep it in our pockets. Does God really need our money? (Yes!) After church, does a big hand come down from heaven and take all the money from the offering plates? (No!)

God wants us to set apart some offerings for him. Do you get an allowance? Get paid for doing odd jobs? Get money as gifts? God has made it possible for you to get the money. He wants us to happily help others and spread the good news of Jesus. One of those ways is with our offerings for the Lord's work.

God loves a cheerful giver.

2 CORINTHIANS 9:7

ARE LITTLE LIES A BIG PROBLEM?

Pretend you're playing kickball. Your team is in the field. The bases are loaded with two outs. The game is tied. It's the last inning. The ball is kicked to you and you chase one of the runners. You reach out with the ball and miss tagging him by a tiny, little bit. But you say you tagged him. You don't want to lose. Is it okay that you said you tagged him, when you really didn't? It's just a silly game. It's just a little lie.

You probably know that lies and cheating are wrong—even a little lie in a little game. If you're going to lie about little things, you're going to find it easy to lie about bigger things.

Check out this verse:

Suppose you can be trusted with very little. Then you can be trusted with a lot. But suppose you are not honest with very little. Then you will not be honest with a lot.

LUKE 16:10 NIrV

Think about that tonight when you lie—down in bed, that is!

275

Persecuted Christians

Jesus said:

> Greater love has no one than this,
> that he lay down his life for his friends.
>
> JOHN 15:13

The Bible also says:

> Stand firm in what you believe. All over
> the world you know that your brothers and sisters
> are going through the same kind of suffering.
>
> 1 PETER 5:9 NIrV

In many countries there are people being killed and tortured because they believe in Jesus Christ! It's happening to kids your age, too!

We need to pray for all who believe in Jesus but live in a place that says they can't! They have many needs. We should be praying that:

➡ they are able to keep their faith and not give in to pressure.
➡ the people who want to hurt or kill them will come to Christ.
➡ the Christians would be safe.
➡ they would use their faith to bring others to know Jesus as their Savior.

What else can you pray about?

276

WHY DO SO MANY GOOD THINGS HAPPEN TO MEAN KIDS?

That girl makes fun of me and talks about me behind my back. But she gets to live in that big house with a swimming pool. That's not fair!

That kid tells the teacher on me when I didn't do anything wrong. He gets his way in everything. He's so popular. He doesn't even believe in God. Why should he get his way?

It's easy to think like that. Since we believe in Jesus Christ as our Savior and it shows through the way we are nice and kind to others, shouldn't we get a reward? Why do mean kids get good things?

Remember:

> The eyes of the LORD are everywhere. They watch those who are evil and those who are good.
>
> PROVERBS 15:3 NIrV

God knows all of our hearts. There is a reward for those who love him as their Savior. We will receive all of it in heaven one day. Maybe he wants to use you to help change those mean kids to God's kids!

WHERE DID YOU LEARN TO LEAN?

Here's the deal with this Dr. Devo's lickety-split devotion—the whole time this is being read, everyone has to lean. Lean whatever direction you want. Ready? Go.

I'm curious to know if everyone is leaning the same way? Different ways? You could be leaning to the right or left, backward or forward. Anyone leaning on someone else? Are you leaning on something? I wish I could see you!

But even though I can't see you, God can see! He knows the direction you're leaning and if you're leaning on something or someone. He also knows how much time you spend leaning on him!

Here's a trick. Try leaning on yourself. Actually, we do that a lot. We lean on ourselves for help instead of leaning on—trusting in—God.

The Bible says:

> Trust in the LORD with all your heart and lean not on your own understanding.
> **PROVERBS 3:5**

Talk about what this verse means. And then straighten up, everyone—while God's Spirit teaches you to learn how to lean on Jesus!

There's an old story that says if you ever see a turtle on top of a fence post, you can be certain that someone put him there. Turtles can't climb their way to the top of a post.

There is a true story that says if a person is in heaven, you can be certain that someone put him or her there. That's the truth. No one can get to heaven alone. So if you want to spend forever in heaven, you have to trust in Jesus as your Savior. And even that trust, or faith, isn't something you created. It's a gift of the Holy Spirit.

> God loves us deeply. He is full of mercy. So he gave us new life because of what Christ has done.... God raised us up with Christ. He has seated us with him in his heavenly kingdom because we belong to Christ Jesus.
>
> EPHESIANS 2:4-6 NIrV

Hey, turtle kids, God raised us up with Christ and sets us in heaven, not on a fence post!

THE SHOW OF SHOWS

If your life were made into a television show, would it be a soap opera, a drama, a sitcom, a game show, or a twenty-four-hour-a-day sports show? What would it be called?

I think that a lot of you think you have a pretty regular, boring life. But I think—and more importantly, God knows—that you have an amazingly exciting, fantabulific, unique, and miraculous life that is the show of all shows. That's because Jesus is part of your life. Jesus said:

> I have come so they can have life. I want them to have it in the fullest possible way.
>
> JOHN 10:10 NIrV

If you think your life is boring, then maybe you're missing all the incredible things going on around you. Maybe you're trying to be the star of your life instead of building your life around Jesus! He wants you to have life in the fullest possible way.

Are you calling your life *Who Wants to Be a Billionaire?* It could be called *I Want to Be with Jesus!*

TICKLING YOURSELF
IS NO FUN

Try to tickle yourself. Did it work? No! Why can others tickle us but we can't tickle ourselves?

Tickling is all about surprise and losing control. When someone is tickling you, most of your time is spent laughing and trying to get away at the same time. There's some danger, but since no one is attacking you in a bad way, your brain thinks it's just fun. Then you start to laugh. That's why you can't tickle yourself. There's no danger or surprise. I guess we'll have to learn to sneak up on ourselves!

Are you ever surprised by God's love? It happens. We human beings just aren't used to being loved the way he loves us.

The Bible says:

> When you sin, the pay you get is death. But God gives you the gift of eternal life because of what Christ Jesus our Lord has done.
>
> ROMANS 6:23 NIrV

What a gift! It's a surprise because we don't deserve it! That should make us smile and even laugh with joy!

Grandparents think grandchildren rock! Okay, they probably don't talk like that, but grandparents love having grandchildren. I hope you have had the opportunity to get to know and love on your grandparents!

The book of Proverbs says:

> Grandchildren are like a crown to older people.
>
> PROVERBS 17:6 NIrV

Take this time to talk about ways that you can share some love with your grandparents this week. If your grandparents are living in heaven already, then pick someone who is "grandparent age" and think of some things you can do to make his or her day.

Here are some ideas.

➡ Write a note (and not on a computer—but with your own, real handwriting!).
➡ Send a care package.
➡ Call and tell your grandparents the reasons you think they rock your world!
➡ Buy or rent a video they would enjoy (and then watch it with them)!
➡ What other ideas can you think of?

GOD—THE ARTIST!

A Sunday school teacher asked her students what they knew about God. A hand shot up in the air. "He's an artist!" said a little boy.

"Really? How do you know that?" the teacher asked.

"You know," the boy said, "our Father, who does art in heaven."

An artist, huh? Well, in a way. Have you seen one of those incredible sunsets he's painted? He has sculpted you. Yes, you are a masterpiece! His "artwork" is all around us.

Read how David talked about the artwork of God:

> LORD, our Lord, how majestic is your name in the whole earth! You have made your glory higher than the heavens. You have made sure that children and infants praise you.... I think about the heavens. I think about what your fingers have created. I think about the moon and stars that you have set in place.... LORD, our Lord, how majestic is your name in the whole earth!
>
> PSALM 8:1-3, 9 NIrV

BOO! DID I SCARE IT OUT OF YOU?

Hic! I can't believe I have the hiccups while I'm (hic!) writing this. This is annoy(hic!)ing! I heard that the word hiccup is short for hiccoughing. (Hic!) That kind of explains what a hiccup is. (Hic!) It's a reflex inside your (hic!) body—like coughing or sneezing. Some(hic!)thing inside you is hugging you (hic!) until you hic it up!

So how do you (hic!) get rid of hiccups? Sometimes a loud "Boo!" can scare the extra breath out of you. The surprise of the (hic!) scare distracts your nervous system, and (hic!) it "forgets" to hiccup. Sometimes you have to just wait until (hic!) your hiccups want to stop!

The devil likes to annoy us. He thinks we don't know the secret to getting rid of him—but we do. All we have to do is call on Jesus to run him off. When Jesus was tempted, he said:

> **Get away from me, Satan!**
> **MATTHEW 4:10 NIrV**

Those are words we can use to scare Satan away, too! Hey, no more hics!

WHAT MAKES A GOOD FRIEND?

We all want good friends, and we want to be a good friend to others. If you are wondering how to make new friends, think about what Jesus said:

> In everything, do to others what you would want them to do to you.
>
> MATTHEW 7:12 NIrV

Here's an assembly kit idea for a good friend.

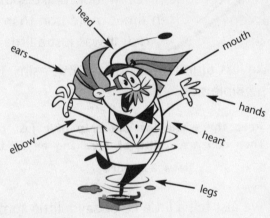

- ➡ listens to you (ears)
- ➡ smart to choose good friends (head)
- ➡ makes you smile (mouth)
- ➡ sees you for who you are and still likes you (eyes)
- ➡ cares about you (heart)
- ➡ laughs with you, not at you (mouth)
- ➡ loves Jesus (heart)
- ➡ flexible—doesn't insist on his or her own way (elbow)
- ➡ willing to help you (hands)
- ➡ plays games with you (legs)

OOPS! IT WAS JUST A LITTLE MISTAKE

Have you heard of the old cartoon Popeye? He got strength from eating spinach. People thought spinach made you stronger because it has lots of iron in it.

That was a mistake! Spinach has no more iron in it than any other green veggie! Back in the 1950s someone made a little mistake in figuring how much iron was in spinach. The decimal point was off by one place. It looked like spinach had ten times more iron than it really did! It was just a little mistake!

Oops! We make lots of little mistakes—"little" sins. No big deal, right? The Bible says:

Suppose you keep the whole law but trip over just one part of it. Then you are guilty of breaking all of it.

JAMES 2:10 NIrV

Wow! Even if we just tell a little lie or say a little something hurtful, we have broken all God's law! Every sin is a big problem, but thankfully we have an even bigger Savior who forgives all who come to him!

TOO LICKED TO LICKITY-SPLIT

We've been lickety-splittin' a long time! I hope you've learned to hold fast to your Savior and his Word. Are you worn out? Tired?

Let's take a deep breath, calm down, and listen to what Jesus says:

> Come to me, all of you who are tired and are carrying heavy loads. I will give you rest. Become my servants and learn from me. I am gentle and free of pride. You will find rest for your souls.
>
> MATTHEW 11:28-29 NIrV

Our lives are so busy! Let's take Jesus up on his great offer! Take time to come to him. Lay your backpacks, basketballs, music books, outfits, packages, and sins at his feet. He has a resting place for everyone who is too licked to lickety-split. Drink from his water fountain of living water. Snuggle up with him and take a nap. Let him read to you from the best book in the whole world—his Book! Take a break with Jesus. He loves you more than you can imagine!

Lickety-split love in Jesus,

Dr. Devo

A big Dr. Devo "Happy New Year!" to you and your family! Yahoo! Yippie! You look tired! Stay up too late last night?

Guess what? Now you have to get used to writing a new year date on your papers at school. Are you one of those people who ruin at least three erasers every January removing the last year's date? Sometimes frustrations come with change.

Let's save our erasers by getting the new year into our heads! Everyone say the new year out loud, slowly but with feeling, ten times. Now say it another ten times as fast as you can.

Sometimes the littlest change can mess us up. Isn't it great to know that the God who erases all our sins, through forgiveness, does not change? He says that in the book of Malachi.

1 the LORD do not change.
MALACHI 3:6

Remember that as you live through changes and any frustrations they bring. May your unchanging Savior bring you joy—in one year and out the other! Yippie! Yahoo! Celebrate God every day!

MARTIN LUTHER KING JR. DAY

Martin Luther King Jr. gave a famous talk in 1963 known as the "I Have a Dream" speech. Part of his dream was that his children would live in a nation where they would be judged by their character rather than the color of their skin. He wanted us to remember that all people are created equal.

Part of God's dream is that all people respect each other as equals and as individuals uniquely created by him. We are not going to be best friends with everyone, but we are called to love all people as we love ourselves.

If you were going to write a speech titled "I Have a Dream of Hope for the Future," what would it be about? How can you help make that dream come true? How did Dr. King work to keep his dream alive? What can you do to keep alive Jesus' dream, which he expressed in the following command?

> Love your neighbor as yourself.
> MARK 12:31

What other dreams does Jesus have for you and your family?

VALENTINE'S DAY

It's time for Dr. Devo's Valentine card-making class! Everyone gets a piece of paper, preferably red (but any color will do). Also needed: scissors, marker or pen, and a stick of gum.

Cut the paper into the shape of a heart. Then cut two slits, near one another, in the middle of the heart, large enough to hold the stick of gum. Write on the heart, around the gum, "I 'chews' you to be my Valentine!" Now you can give it to the Valentine of your choice.

If Jesus gave out Valentine cards, it could say that, too. He might add a cross to remind us of how much he loves us. We didn't choose Jesus; he chose us. He might also write, "John 15:16–17." That's where Jesus said:

> You did not choose me, but I chose you and appointed you to go and bear fruit—fruit that will last.... This is my command: Love each other.

Every day is a Valentine's Day when we live in his love and care.

PRESIDENTS' DAY

Although Presidents' Day falls between the birthdays of Presidents Lincoln and Washington, it's a day to remember all who have held that office. Here's some lickety-split presidential trivia.

- → James Madison was the shortest president at five feet, four inches.
- → Lincoln was the tallest at six feet, four inches.
- → The teddy bear was named for Theodore (Teddy) Roosevelt.
- → Thomas Jefferson, John Adams, and James Monroe all died on July Fourth.
- → In 1976 President Gerald Ford sent out forty thousand Christmas cards.
- → President John Tyler had fifteen children.

This isn't trivia but God's Word:

> Everyone must submit himself to the governing authorities, for there is no authority except that which God has established. The authorities that exist have been established by God.
>
> **ROMANS 13:1**

What does this verse mean to your family? Our government and all its leaders need our prayers. Keep praying for all our government leaders.

FOUR DAYS BEFORE EASTER (WEDNESDAY)

The Bible doesn't say how Jesus spent the Wednesday before Easter—two days before he would be crucified. The Sunday before, he rode into Jerusalem on a donkey. We call that day Palm Sunday. On Monday he cleared the moneychangers from the temple. On Tuesday he spent time teaching people. On Thursday he celebrated the Passover meal with his disciples and gave them the Lord's Supper (Communion), then prayed in the Garden of Gethsemane, and later was arrested for a crime he didn't commit. On Friday he was crucified and died. On Saturday he was in the tomb. And on Sunday he rose from the dead.

What do you think he did on Wednesday? If you knew you were going to die in two days, what might you do? Talk about that with your family.

My thoughts are that he spent time alone, praying to his heavenly Father. Let's follow up on that thought by spending extra time in prayer today. Quiet prayer time might be just what you need to get through the rest of this week.

THREE DAYS BEFORE EASTER (THURSDAY)

If you had to do all but one of the following things, what would you leave off your list?

- → set the table for dinner
- → wish your neighbor, "Happy birthday!"
- → help a friend with homework
- → vacuum your bedroom
- → wash your friend's dirty feet

I'm guessing it didn't take you long to decide (although you might have paused for a while to think hard about vacuuming your room). Those are all ways of serving others. But washing someone's dirty, smelly feet? Would you? Could you?

Jesus did! The night before he was crucified, he met with his disciples in the upper room of a home to celebrate the Passover meal and talk to them before his death. One thing he wanted to teach them was to find joy in serving others, the way he was a servant. That night Jesus had them take off their sandals and he washed their dusty feet. What a lesson to us to serve others as he served us all!

TWO DAYS BEFORE EASTER (GOOD FRIDAY)

Here's a simple Dr. Devo crossword puzzles with a powerful message to think about and talk about on this special day when Jesus died for us.

```
        f
        o
        r
        g
        i
Savior
        e
        n
        e
        s
        s
```

1 across: Jesus is my _____ who died on the cross to give me forgiveness for all my sins and eternal life.

1 down: Jesus is my Savior who died on the cross to give me _____ for all my sins and eternal life.

A family discussion and prayer about the meaning of Jesus' cross and his "cross" words of life would be very appropriate, don't you think?

ONE DAY BEFORE EASTER (SATURDAY)

Question: Do you know why cemeteries have fences around them?

Answer: Because so many people are dying to get into them!

Jesus was dying to get into a tomb owned by a man named _____. Remember? (If not, check out Matthew 27:57–61.) Jesus was dying to get there for us! He was dying to get there so he could finish the mission his Father had sent him to accomplish.

Even David, who lived way before Jesus, trusted God's promises about the grave. He wrote:

> My heart is glad and my tongue rejoices; my body also will rest secure, because you will not abandon me to the grave.
>
> PSALM 16:9-10

God didn't leave his son Jesus in the grave, and he won't leave our bodies there, either. With that good news, enjoy whatever you are "dying" to do this weekend!

Jesus lives! The tomb is empty!

(This page is pretty empty, too! Share your own lickety-split devotion about what the emptiness of the tomb means to you!)

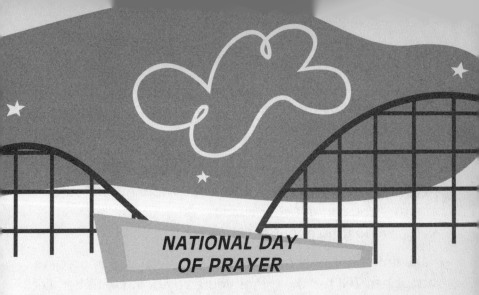

NATIONAL DAY OF PRAYER

To pray or play, that is the question. That is Dr. Devo's question on this National Day of Prayer. I'm going to challenge you to give up some or all of your playtime today (or tomorrow, if you don't have any more playtime today). In place of playing, pray—or while playing, pray.

You don't have to sit in a chair at recess, hands folded and head bowed. Take a walk around the playground while talking to God. Or swing while silently singing God's praise in prayer. When you get home after school, ride your bike while praying. Pray for our nation and its leaders. Pray that God would guide our leaders as the book of Proverbs says:

> For lack of guidance a nation falls,
> but many advisers make victory sure.
> **PROVERBS 11:14**

Also take time to praise God for who he is, thanking him for the incredible, amazing love he has for you!

Praying instead of playing. It's a small sacrifice when we consider the life-giving sacrifice Jesus made for us. What and who will you be praying for?

MOTHER'S DAY

Question: What is a coat?

Answer: It is something your mother makes you wear when she is cold!

Mothers are special gifts. They have special hearts for their children. One mother once wrote this for other moms: "You can get your children off your lap, but you can never get them out of your heart."

Take time right now to tell your mom what you appreciate about her. Tell her the things you enjoy doing with her. Let her know what you appreciate about her faith. Then get all mushy and give her a nice, wet kiss—right in her ear! She'll love it! (I hope!)

Some of you have mothers who aren't in your home with you on Mother's Day. Some are living in heaven, and others live in another home, state, or country. Please know that those of us reading this are going to say a special prayer for you today! You are loved!

Thank you, Lord, for moms! Bless and strengthen them in their high calling! Amen.

ASCENSION

Most people don't spend time thinking about Jesus' ascension into heaven. It is a Thursday, forty days after Jesus rose from the dead. Stop now and read Acts 1:1–11 to learn about that day.

It must have been exciting for Jesus to return to his Father. When was a time you couldn't wait to get home? It must have been a sad time for his disciples. They would really miss him. I want you to do something the disciples did: Everyone stare at the ceiling (or the sky if you're outside). Keep doing that for about one minute or until you feel pretty silly!

Now give your neck a break and stop looking up! What did the angels say to the disciples when they were staring into the sky? The angels were trying to point the disciples to the day when Jesus would return.

Since necks might be sore, give each other a neck massage while saying, "God loves you and is coming back to take you home."

Name as many pieces of fire-fighting equipment as you can in one minute—anything that helps put out a fire. Someone watch the clock. Ready, set, go!

Name ways the Holy Spirit "fires up" God's people to grow in their relationship with Jesus. Someone watch the clock. Go!

Name ways people put out the faith-growing fires that the Holy Spirit has started. Someone watch the clock. Ready? Go!

The day of Pentecost is remembered fifty days after Jesus rose from the dead—that is, ten days after his ascension into heaven. I would encourage you to read the story (Acts 2) of what happened as people came from all over to celebrate this harvest festival.

It's a day when we remember the gift of the Holy Spirit. He "fires" us up through the hearing of God's Word, through baptism, through the Lord's Supper, and through other ways you may have mentioned. We also need to remember what Paul wrote:

Do not put out the Spirit's fire.
1 THESSALONIANS 5:19

Blaze, Spirit, blaze! We want to be fired up for Jesus!

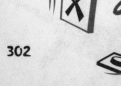

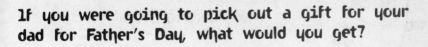

FATHER'S DAY

If you were going to pick out a gift for your dad for Father's Day, what would you get?

- a really cool tie
- a tool
- a card
- a really ugly tie
- something you made (for free)
- something from the dollar store

It can be hard to decide what to give your father. But it's not difficult to see what has been given to you.

Being blessed with a Christian dad is a wonderful gift you receive on Father's Day! And having the perfect heavenly Father with you always is an incredible gift for which you can always be thankful!

Some of you have fathers who aren't in your home with you today. Some are living in heaven, and others live in another home, state, or country. Please know that those of us reading this are going to say a special prayer for you today! You are loved!

Thank you, God, for dads everywhere! Help them to learn about fatherhood from you, the perfect Father! Amen.

MEMORIAL DAY

What did you eat for lunch last Tuesday? Can you remember three gifts you got for Christmas? How did you spend the day before your birthday?

Can't remember? But this is Memorial Day—a day to remember! It's easy to forget things. Actually, Memorial Day is a day to honor the men and women who gave their lives in service to our country, both in peace and in times of war.

We need to be thankful for those servicemen and servicewomen, never forgetting what they did for us. We also never want to forget what Jesus did by giving his life so we can have a free life both here on earth and also in heaven!

Remembering the battles and the ones doing battle, pay attention to what David said before he fought Goliath:

> It is not by sword or spear that the LORD saves;
> for the battle is the LORD's.
>
> 1 SAMUEL 17:47

LABOR DAY

What job would you like to have someday?

Dr. Devo has had a lot of jobs. I was a firefighter for a while—until I got fired! Would it shock you to know that I was an electrician? Watt? You don't believe me? I tried to set up a branch office as a lumberjack, but I was stumped by all the questions people asked. I lost interest in my job at a bank. At a computer store, I had to monitor the workers until someone got upgraded to my job and I was deleted from the business.

I didn't have enough patients to be a dentist or doctor. I tried to get a job as a cartoon character at an amusement park in Florida, but they said I was too goofy! But now God has led me to be a Christian writer for a spell!

Whatever job God leads you to, don't forget these words:

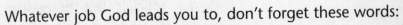

> Serve wholeheartedly, as if you
> were serving the Lord, not men.
>
> EPHESIANS 6:7

ELECTION DAY

It seems to me there was a band called the Seven Dwarfs that had a hit song called, "I Owe, I Owe, It's Off to Vote I Go!" That could be a good song for Election Day. Maybe the words to the song could be from the book of Romans:

> Authorities are God's servants, who give their full time to governing. Give everyone what you owe him: If you owe taxes, pay taxes; if revenue, then revenue; if respect, then respect; if honor, then honor.
>
> ROMANS 13:6-7

Those words don't have much of a beat or rhythm, but they are good words to remember—even if you're not old enough to vote! God has created our government as a system in which people serve over us. We want to pray that the nation will elect people who will follow God's will.

We owe respect and honor to our elected officials, but the greater law that governs us is God's. Pray today that all elected officials will obey God's will and pass that on to our country.

THANKSGIVING DAY

Happy Thanksgiving from Dr. Devo! Every year we thank God for our blessings and especially for the gift of Jesus, our Savior. Are most of your prayers of thanksgiving basically the same? It's great to thank God for faith, family, friends, and food (the four big Fs). This year add things you have never mentioned before. There are critters, creatures, and characters (the three big Cs) that all serve a purpose for which we rarely give him thanks. I'll start and everyone can add to the list.

Thank you, God, for sending Jesus Christ into this world and into our lives to save us, forgive us, and change us. Thank you for all your blessings, including worms that wiggle and cartoons that make us giggle, moles that dig and every smelly ol' pig, and (oh, do I have to say it?) snakes and spiders and lizards, too!

Add your thanksgivings here:

_____

_____

_____

_____

Give thanks in all circumstances.

1 THESSALONIANS 5:18

We'll be back to our regularly scheduled program after this commercial for Dr. Devo's Advent Colanders.

[Note to those reading this devotion: Use a different, fun voice for the commercial.]

Announcer: Hello, boys and girls! It's almost Christmas, but it's not too late for you to get a Dr. Devo Advent Colander. That's right, I said colander, not calendar!

What's a colander, you ask? It's just a fancy name for one of those spaghetti strainers you probably have in your kitchen. What's the purpose of one of those strainers, or colanders? To get rid of the water and keep the noodles—the important part! That's what a Dr. Devo Advent Colander can remind you of. There is so much stuff that comes with Christmas that the world thinks is important but isn't. Let go of that stuff and keep the true meaning of Christmas, and that is:

Christ Jesus came into the world to save sinners.

1 TIMOTHY 1:15

To get one, call 1-555-MOM-WHERE'S-OUR-COLANDER?

Now back to our regularly scheduled program, "How to Make Reindeer Soup."

We'll be back to our regularly scheduled program after another commercial from our sponsor, Dr. Devo's Advent Colanders.

Announcer: Hello, boys and girls! Everyone is talking about the Dr. Devo Advent Colanders. Today I'm here to tell you about another way you can use yours. We've already encouraged you to use it to strain out the unwanted parts of the world's Christmas celebration. Now think about setting your colander (without noodles in it) wherever your family eats. Have each family member write prayer requests, pantomime ideas, or Bible readings on small slips of paper and toss them into the colander.

You could write things like, "Pantomime the angels telling the shepherds of Jesus' birth" or "How many carols can you think of that have the word *joy* in the title?" or "Read Luke 2:1–20" or "Pray for Grandma and Grandpa." Daily, each family member can pick out a slip of paper and do what it says. Have fun!

THREE DAYS BEFORE CHRISTMAS

Here's a Dr. Devo Christmas quiz! This should be easy, right?

- How did Mary and Joseph travel to Bethlehem (for example: by foot, donkey, bus, etc.)?
- What animals were present at Jesus' birth?
- Where was Jesus born (for example: stable, cave, hotel)?
- How many wise men (Magi) came to worship Jesus?

Most information about Jesus' birth can be found in Luke 2 or Matthew 2. But the idea of Joseph walking while Mary rode a donkey isn't. There may have been animals present at Jesus' birth, since there was a manger (a feeding trough for animals), but the Bible doesn't say. A stable is never mentioned. And although three gifts were given by the wise men, the Bible never says how many Magi worshiped Jesus.

Animals, stables, or three wise men may not seem like a big deal. But problems can arise when we don't check to see exactly what the Bible says. So read those two chapters and see how many facts about Christmas you can confirm.

TWO DAYS
BEFORE CHRISTMAS

Dr. Devo has a fun project for the next few devotions. We're going to try to fill in the blanks that tell the story of Jesus' birth. The answers are found in Luke 2. Here are the first seven verses.

In those days Caesar _____ issued a decree that a _____ should be taken of the entire Roman world. [This was the first _____ that took place while Quirinius was governor of Syria.] And everyone went to his own _____ to register. So _____ also went up from the town of _____ in Galilee to Judea, to _____ the town of _____, because he belonged to the house and _____ of _____. He went there to register with _____, who was pledged to be _____ to him and was expecting a _____. While they were there, the time came for the _____ to be _____, and she gave birth to her _____, a _____. She _____ him in _____ and placed him in a _____, because there was no _____ for them in the _____.

LUKE 2:1-7

Let's continue where we left off with yesterday's devotion, filling in the blanks that tell the story of Jesus' birth.

And there were _____ living out in the _____ nearby, keeping watch over their _____ at night. An _____ of the _____ appeared to them, and the _____ of the Lord shone around them, and they were _____. But the _____ said to them, "Do not be _____. I bring you _____ _____ of _____ _____ that will be for all the people. Today in the town of David a _____ has been born to you; he is _____ the _____. This will be a _____ to you: You will find a baby wrapped in _____ and lying in a _____."
Suddenly a great company of the heavenly _____ appeared with the _____, praising God and saying, "Glory to _____ in the _____, and on earth _____ to men on whom his favor rests."
LUKE 2:8-14

Celebrate with the angels that surround your house tonight!

Merry Christmas! My prayer is that you are having great fun celebrating Jesus' birth! Let's continue to fill in the blanks that tell of his birth.

When the _____ had left them and gone into _____, the _____ said to one another, "Let's _____ to _____ and see this thing that has happened, which the _____ has told us about."
So they _____ off and found _____ and _____, and the _____, who was lying in the _____. When they had seen him, they spread the _____ concerning what had been told them about this _____, and all who heard it were _____ at what the _____ said to them. But Mary _____ up all these things and _____ them in her _____. The shepherds returned, glorifying and _____ God for all the things they had _____ and _____, which were just as they had been _____.
LUKE 2:15-20

Just as Mary treasured up and pondered all the events of Jesus' birth, may we all do the same. With that thought, have a "*Mary* kind of Christmas!"

ONE DAY AFTER CHRISTMAS

I hope you had a wonderful celebration of our Savior's birth! What a gift you got! No, I'm not talking about the three-pack of socks and underwear under the tree. I'm talking about the gift of Jesus under the tree—the tree shaped like a cross. Jesus came to earth with the purpose of going to the cross to die for our sins so we could be saved. He also came to rise from the dead so we can live forever with him!

Think about the gifts that Jesus brings to your life, like:

- forgiveness
- hope
- self-control
- joy
- salvation
- wisdom
- peace
- faithfulness
- love
- help
- compassion
- strength
- freedom
- comfort

Can you think of some more gifts that come with Jesus? How about your family and friends? Rejoice in the gift of Jesus that keeps on giving and will never end!

> Today in the town of David a Savior
> has been born to you; he is Christ the Lord.
>
> LUKE 2:11

TWO DAYS AFTER CHRISTMAS

Did you hang Christmas stockings in your house? I don't know where that idea came from. But it's a good way to get extra goodies! I like it for another reason. Here's why, in the form of a short poem:

My stockings were hung by the chimney with care.
I had worn them for months and they needed the air!
Would they be filled with goodies—all but the kitchen sink—
Or would they be empty again because so bad was the stink?

It would stink if we didn't get any stocking stuffers because our socks stunk! It would also stink if God had decided not to send us the gift of Jesus because our lives were all smelly from sin.

Thankfully, Jesus did come to wash away our sins with his cleansing forgiveness! What a gift! Listen to these words from a dirty sinner:

Wash away all my iniquity and cleanse me from my sin....
Cleanse me ... and 1 will be clean; wash me,
and 1 will be whiter than snow.

PSALM 51:2, 7

Hey, wise guys and girls out there, did you know that the wise men, or Magi, didn't visit Jesus for probably six months to two years after Jesus' birth? On January 6 we remember their visit. It's a day called Epiphany.

If you have a Nativity set, here's an idea for you. (If you don't have one, draw a picture of some wise guys—I mean, wise men—and, on a separate piece of paper, a picture of baby Jesus.) Since the wise men came from a long way away, place them across the room from the Nativity set (or picture of Jesus). Every day leading up to January 6, move them closer to Jesus. On January 6 read how they worshiped Jesus in Matthew 2:1–12.

Each day when you move them closer, you can worship Jesus by praying, "Move me closer to you, Jesus."

> On coming to the house,
> [the wise men] saw the child
> with his mother Mary, and they
> bowed down and worshiped him.
>
> MATTHEW 2:11

Today you get to act out the role of the weatherperson on TV. It's going to be your show, so you're on your own. You'll need to tell your audience the current temperature and what the weather is going to be like for the rest of the day and tomorrow. You can even tell them what you think the weather is like in other parts of the country. Whenever you're ready, go for it! (And feel free to ham it up!)

It's time for the weather . . . [That's you!]

Great job! Channel 5 should be contacting you next week about a possible job! Now check out this weather report—Jesus tells us that no matter where we live as the time draws closer to his return, one of the signs will be:

> Because of the increase of wickedness, the love of most will grow cold, but he who stands firm to the end will be saved.
>
> MATTHEW 24:12-13

Ask Jesus to always keep your heart warm with his love.

FIVE DAYS AFTER CHRISTMAS

Only 360-ish more shopping days till Christmas! Yippie. Yahoo. Blah, blah, blah. Bored with Christmas already? Are you sick of eating Christmas leftovers? Are you tired of looking at the sagging ol' tree? Don't want to hear one more Christmas carol? Hey! What's up with that? The message of Christmas—Jesus coming to earth to save us— is a message for the whole year! It's a message of joy! So here's your assignment: Take each letter of the word *Christmas* and write a word of joy and celebration connected with Jesus' birth.

Before you do, check out Mary's joyful words when she found out she was giving birth to the Savior.

**My soul glorifies the Lord
and my spirit rejoices in God my Savior.**
LUKE 1:46-47

Continue to have a "Mary" Christmas!

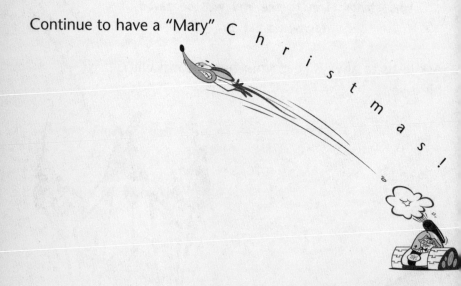

NEW YEAR'S EVE

Let's make a Dr. Devo end-of-the-year journal.

Thinking back over the past year, answer the following:

→ What or who did you pray about most this year?
→ What and who are you especially thankful for?
→ What Bible verse or story was especially helpful?
→ What was the saddest thing about this year?
→ What was the best blessing you received?
→ What was something really funny that happened ?
→ What is your favorite devotional book you used this year? (You'd better get this right!)
→ What helped you grow closer to God, your family, and/or your church family?
→ How did God use you to help others?

It's the last day of the year. Here's the last verse of the Bible, and it's Dr. Devo's prayer for you, as a special gift within God's family.

The grace of the Lord Jesus be with God's people. Amen.
REVELATION 22:21

God's grace (his undeserved love) is with you—in one year and out the other!

We want to hear from you. Please send your comments about this
book to us in care of the address below. Thank you.

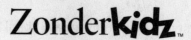

Grand Rapids, MI 49530
www.zonderkidz.com